BOUND BY FIRE

By
ELIZABETH SINCLAIR

DEDICATION

To those brave men and women who make up the Adirondack Forest Rangers.

Having spent my honeymoon there, I can't forget the beauty and grandeur of the mountains and woodlands that make up New York State's Adirondack Mountains.

Thank you for watching over it.

Bound By Fire
Table of Contents

CHAPTER 1 1

CHAPTER 2 12

CHAPTER 3 22

CHAPTER 4 35

CHAPTER 5 43

CHAPTER 6 54

CHAPTER 7 64

CHAPTER 8 70

CHAPTER 9 78

CHAPTER 10 87

CHAPTER 11 95

CHAPTER 12 105

CHAPTER 13 114

CHAPTER 14 126

CHAPTER 15 134

CHAPTER 16 141

CHAPTER 17 151

EPILOGUE...166

PREVIEW:
THE SURVIVORS

BLOOD ON THE ASHES 173

ABOUT THE AUTHOR...175

ABOUT THE COVER DESIGNER 177

Chapter 1

"I've been a complete ass." Karen Ellis glanced apprehensively across the dining room table at her older sister, Elle Banks.

"Yes, you have." Elle softened the accusation with a smile. "Want to tell me why?"

Elle's birthday party guests had left hours earlier and there was no longer any way Karen could escape the inevitable explanation that had waited years to be put into words.

Nervous about how Elle would take her admission of guilt, Karen put off explaining by repeatedly running a piece of yellow ribbon between her thumb and forefinger. As it slid between her fingers, the ribbon's curl became tighter and tighter, until it mirrored Karen's coiled nerves. Needing no reminders of how much the mere thought of having this conversation had crawled under her skin, Karen threw the ribbon back in the pile of torn and crumpled wrapping paper, empty gift boxes, and mangled bows littering the table.

"Well?" Elle prompted.

Karen glanced at Elle. Even though Elle pressed her for an answer, Karen could tell from her sister's guarded expression that she had no more desire to open the door to their very painful past than Karen did. The uncomfortable silence of two strangers trying to find common ground enveloped them.

Elle finally looked up, determination evident in her set mouth. "What happened to us, Karen? We were close once, when we were little. When did it all fall apart?"

Karen took a deep fortifying breath. No matter how difficult and no matter what the consequences, the time had come to clean the slate and finally be honest with both herself and Elle.

"I guess it started when I began blaming you for Dad walking out on us and Mom's need for fame by living vicariously through you and, in the process, forgetting she had two daughters." Karen looked away, ashamed now of how long she'd allowed her petty, misplaced blame to stand between them. "But you were as much a victim as I was." She shrugged. "Maybe more so. After having a long talk with Dad today at the party, I understand why he left. It couldn't have been easy for him watching Mom steal our childhood by treating me like a stepchild and dragging you from beauty pageant to beauty pageant."

All the years of loneliness that had burned inside her seemed to melt away with each word she spoke. She pushed on.

"You were the shining star, and I became the invisible child. Elle's hanger-on sister. Mom's unwanted burden. Somewhere along the way, I began to resent you for it. It wasn't until years later that I realized that Mom never gave you a choice. But by that time, I didn't know how to fix it between us." Her eyes burned with unshed tears. "Can we fix it?" She blinked the tears away and met her sister's gaze. "Can we?"

"Isn't that what we're doing?" Elle smiled and squeezed Karen's hand. "It's in the past, sweetie. If I've learned anything in the last few months, it's that we have to let the past rest and not taint today. Life is too short for should-haves. Sometimes we're so busy worrying about what was that we miss out on what can be."

Emotion clogging her throat, Karen could only nod. She didn't think she deserved Elle's forgiveness, but she was infinitely glad that she'd given it, especially now. Never had she needed her sister more.

"The Ellis sisters are reunited, so where are the smiles?" Tilting her head, Elle frowned. "Could it be because burying the hatchet wasn't the only thing that brought you here?"

"Not entirely. Truth is, I'm—" Karen swallowed hard, summoning the courage to let go of her precious secret.

Elle got up and came around the table. She drew up a chair

beside Karen and put her arm around her sister's shoulders. "You're what?" She waited, but Karen still couldn't find the words. "Come on. We're sisters. Sisters share." Elle laid her forehead against Karen's. "Remember how we used to whisper our secrets to each other after Mom and Dad went to bed?"

Unable to force words past the clog of emotion in her throat, Karen nodded.

Her sister squeezed her hand again. "Well, I'm still willing to be your confidante."

Karen raised her head. "You're the best."

Responding with a grin and a wink, Elle looked happier than Karen could remember ever seeing her. "That's what Scott tells me."

The all too familiar ache of loneliness that had squeezed her heart for the last three months grew inside Karen. Elle was so lucky to have Scott. Her handsome detective husband doted on her, and anyone with eyes in their head could see the depth of his love for his wife.

"Elle, I'm pregnant."

The words tumbled out before Karen could stop them, but as she'd said them, she'd felt the tension drain from her body. Until that very moment, she hadn't realized how much it had been costing her to carry this burden alone.

Elle's mouth fell open. Surprise and delight danced across her features. Then she hugged Karen. "That's wonderful. When are you due? What about your husband? I didn't even know you'd gotten marr—" Elle leaned closer and studied Karen for a long moment. "Why do I get the feeling that you're not a happy mother-to-be?"

Sunshine sifted through the window and beat down on Karen's cold, tightly clenched hands. Amazed that talking about this could still hurt so much, she reached deep down inside and summoned the words of explanation. "I'm thrilled about the baby, but . . . I'm not married, Elle. The baby's father, Paul Jackson, died three months ago in a forest fire in upstate New York." Old pain muffled the last few words. She cleared her throat of emotion. "He didn't know about the baby. Aside from my doctor and now you, no one else knows."

Smoothing her hand over her flat stomach, Karen couldn't help but smile. At three and half months, she should have at least had a small potbelly, but she wasn't showing yet, which had helped her keep her secret. The loss of weight she'd suffered from morning sickness and the shock of Paul's death had kept her pregnancy concealed from everyone but her doctor. And that's the way she'd wanted it, until now.

After losing Paul, his child was all she'd had left of him, and she wanted to treasure that for a bit longer. Not having the opportunity to mourn Paul's death in the normal way, the process had been hard for Karen to weather. She'd made it, only by reminding herself of her responsibility to her child. However, when she allowed them admittance, memories of Paul continued to haunt her.

But memories weren't all that haunted her.

"There's something else." Karen grasped Elle's hand in a desperate grip. "I want this baby to have the family we never had. I want to find Paul's family and tell them about the baby. Will you help me?"

Perplexed, Elle stared at Karen. "I don't understand. Why don't you know where his family is? Didn't you meet them at his funeral?"

Memories bombarded Karen again. "I didn't go to Paul's funeral. I didn't even know anything had happened until I called the ranger station to find out why I hadn't heard from him. By that time, Paul had been dead for weeks. The funeral and burial had already been held.

"As for family, Paul and I never discussed his family or mine." She felt the heat of her cheeks pinking slightly. "We only had a few months together, and I guess we were too busy being in love to care about our pasts. Then again, maybe we sensed that neither of us wanted to discuss our families. All I know is that he was from

Montana, and he graduated from Cornell University's School of Forestry where he met Jesse Kingston, his fellow ranger and best friend. I've contacted the university, and they gave me the same runaround as the Adirondack Mountains Preserve's ranger station—it's against policy to give out any personal information."

Elle sighed. "Geeze, Karen, I want to help you, but I'm not sure how." Deep in thought, Elle drummed her fingertips on the tabletop. "What about his friend, this Jesse what's-his-name? Wouldn't he know how to locate Paul's family?"

"Jesse Kingston." Karen sighed. "Another dead-end. When I called to talk to him, he'd just left for home on medical leave, and the ranger station wouldn't give me his address."

A broad grin broke across Elle's face. "Well, I happen to have connections within the firefighting community, and my connections have connections."

She picked up the phone, punched in a number from memory, and waited. "Donna, I need a favor. Can you find the home address for a forest ranger named Jesse Kingston? He's based in upstate New York's Adirondack Mountains Preserve." Elle paused. "I'll explain later, just find it for me as soon as you can, and call me back." She covered the receiver with her hand and turned to Karen. "Do you want her to get Paul's info, too?"

Knowing she hadn't told Elle everything, Karen hesitated for a moment, then shook her head. She *had* to speak to Jesse herself. "This is enough of an imposition. If she can just get Jesse's address, I'm sure, when I talk to him, I can get Paul's information from him."

For a long moment, Elle frowned at her, but finally removed her hand from the receiver. "Okay, Donna, I guess that's it. Thanks. I owe you one." She hung up. "Donna Lawrence is my best friend. She knows people she can contact. She's going to do some digging and get back to me."

Relief washed through Karen. Because it was pure speculation on her part, she hadn't told Elle the other reason for wanting to find Jesse Kingston.

Paul had been a first-class forest ranger, and she was having a hard time believing his death was an accident. She recalled vividly how upset he'd been when he'd related how a new ranger had done something very like what they claimed Paul had done. The young ranger had nearly died for his lack of good judgment.

It didn't make sense that Paul would walked into a wall of fire that he knew would probably kill him. If anyone could tell her why Paul had done something so completely out of character, it would be Jesse.

"The mongrel son returns," Jesse Kingston jeered softly to himself.

He backed his battered, brown SUV into one of the two open parking spots in front of The Diner, his tiny hometown of Bristol's favorite gathering place. Turning off the engine, he glanced first at the array of pick-up trucks and cars crowding the lot, then at his watch. The trip south from the mountains to Bristol should have only taken a little over an hour. If it hadn't been for the weekend traffic, he'd have been here a long time ago.

More to the point, if his boss, Chief Ranger Hank Thompson, hadn't ordered him home to "get his head on straight," Jesse wouldn't be here at all. He'd be in the only place he'd ever considered to be his real home—the forest.

He could still hear Hank's words ringing in his ears. "You're driving everyone around here crazy with your questions about Paul's death. I want the questions to stop, and I want you to go home and get a handle on your life." He'd taken a deep breath and when he spoke again his boss-voice was gone. "Dammit! It's not rocket science, Jesse, and there's no big mystery. The official report was that Jackson stupidly walked into a bad situation and paid the price. We all make mistakes. For your sake and mine, let it go."

Jesse couldn't let it go. Hank was wrong. Paul didn't make mistakes. Jesse had known him ever since they'd graduated from forestry school. They'd been through hell together fighting forest fires shoulder to shoulder. Paul was the best. He'd had risen up the ranks fast and eventually became Jesse's superior officer. But they'd remained friends. Paul had never pulled rank on Jesse until that day three months ago when he'd ordered Jesse to stay behind while he'd walked into the trees and had never come out.

He hadn't told Hank, but just because he was back in Bristol didn't mean he'd stop wondering and stop trying to find out what actually happened to Paul. Before Jesse would find any inner peace, he had to know if it was his fault, if he'd followed Paul would it have made a difference, and would Paul be alive today.

Familiar guilt flooded through him. Jesse rubbed his hand over his tired, burning eyes and wished for the thousandth time that he hadn't obeyed Paul's orders. If he'd just followed him anyway. If he'd—

He cut off the painful musings and let his gaze wander, taking in the lazy street activity. The town hadn't changed much. Elma Davidson, a cane supporting her arthritic body, hobbled toward the library with the latest bestseller tucked under her arm. Marv Adams still had the *For Sale* sign in The Gazette window, right where it had been for twenty years. The Garden Club had planted a colorful array of summer flowers around the flagpole in the center of the small, grassy, town square.

How deceptive it all was. Beneath its lazy, welcoming exterior, Jesse could almost hear the hum of gossip that would begin when the townspeople found out Frank Kingston's son was back. The same gossip mill had worked overtime when Jesse's mother had left his father and then again when Jesse had come back here at the age of nine.

Jesse sighed. Despite the familiar sites and the fact that he'd grown up here, he still felt like a stranger. Would there ever come a time when he thought of this place as home?

He started to open the car door, but hesitated. Did he really want to stay? He could just back the car out and no one would ever know he'd even been there.

You've been running away from things all your life. Isn't it about time you stopped?

Unsure if he was ready to face his childhood demons, Jesse conceded that running hadn't helped before and probably wouldn't help now, but he was here, and he might as well stay. Stuffing his apprehension in his back pocket, Jesse climbed from the car, closed the door, and then went into the diner.

Karen's stomach growled. She hadn't eaten since the Danish and coffee she'd grabbed at a Thruway rest stop hours ago. She leaned into the car, retrieved her purse, closed and locked the door, then headed for the diner. From all the travels with her mother over the years, she'd learned that the hub of any information in a small town was one of two places, the local garage or the local eatery.

Thanks to Elle's friend Donna's connections, Karen knew that Jesse Kingston lived in Bristol, NY. Unfortunately, Donna couldn't get a street address. With any luck, one of the diner's local patrons could provide one.

Just inside, Karen paused and did a double take. From its pink and black vinyl booths to the chrome bands around the counter stools and the rainbow-colored jukebox tucked in the back corner, The Diner looked like it had fallen straight out of an episode of *Happy Days*. The hum of the customers' voices nearly drowned out the strains of a plaintive country song drifting out from the jukebox. The air hung heavy with the smells of used grease, cooking meat, and body odors.

A sign beside the cash register read "Seat Yourself." Since there were quite a few diners, Karen didn't have a big choice. The booths were all taken by several couples, four men loudly discussing the latest baseball scores, and one man sitting alone with his back to her, his attention buried in a newspaper.

She made her way down the narrow aisle between the booths and the counter seats and chose one of the only available stools.

A tall, thirtyish man emerging through a door to her left drew her attention from the small, cardboard menu card she'd pulled from between a napkin holder and a bottle of ketchup.

Over his shoulder, she could see a door with the word *Roosters* and a picture of a rooster in overalls chewing on a piece of straw painted on it.

The man walked down the aisle with the assurance of someone totally at home here. As he progressed toward her, he spoke to several people at the counter and paused to add his opinion of the Yankees last game to those already expressed loud and clear by the group in the booth. Moments later, obviously seeing that he was not going to change anyone's assessment that the Yankees would take the pennant, he shook his head and moved on. He'd almost reached her when he stopped next to the booth occupied by the lone man reading the newspaper.

"Well, I'll be damned. As I live and breathe. If it isn't Jesse Kingston in the flesh."

Jesse glanced up from the newspaper, which he hadn't been really reading, but using more as a shield against anyone attempting to engage him in conversation. Evidently, Charlie Clay didn't let a little thing like a newspaper stand in his way.

"Hello, Charlie."

"When'd you get back in town?"

"Little while ago." Hopefully if he didn't give the appearance of wanting to exchange pleasantries, this conversation would end quickly. Charlie's next words told Jesse he'd been successful.

"Well . . . nice to see you." Charlie edged away.

As the construction worker moved on, Jesse caught sight of the woman at the counter. She faced him and although he couldn't see her eyes, which were hidden behind sunglasses, he could tell she was showing an overt interest in him. Used to his dark looks drawing attention from women, he tried to dismiss her stare. But he couldn't seem to tear his gaze from her.

Jesse didn't recognize her. If this woman had lived in Bristol, he would definitely remember. With that kind of breathtaking beauty, how could he not? Feeling more interest in a woman than he had in sometime, past the one-night-stand stage, Jesse, like the woman staring at him from behind the dark sunglasses, made no effort to hide his blatant appraisal of her.

A cascade of ash blonde curls fell about the shoulders of her snug, green halter-top. Low-slung denim jeans molded her curvy hips, thighs, and endless legs. She removed her sunglasses and brilliant green, questioning eyes gazed back at him.

To his surprise, he felt his breath catch. His chest expanded in an effort to draw in enough oxygen to sustain him. His throat went dry. Jesse felt more life surging through him than he would have believed possible. Still, two questions hammered at his mind.

Who is this gorgeous woman, and why is she staring at me?

When Karen had heard the man's name, her heartbeat sped up. She gasped. Unable to believe her luck, she stared across the narrow aisle at Jesse Kingston. He slid his gaze over her. Rather than seeing it as an insolent gesture, she felt her body warm involuntarily, as though he'd actually made physical contact with her skin. He was probably one of the handsomest men she'd ever recalled encountering. Wind-blown waves of jet-black hair framed his tanned face, and the set of his square jaw proclaimed an unbending nature. For a moment, she tried to visualize his face creased in a smile. The resulting image made her breath catch.

Just stop it, Karen!

But the desolate look in his dark brown eyes had struck a chord inside her. A sharp ache passed through her heart. She knew that look. She'd seen it often enough on her own face while she was growing up. Loneliness. She also knew he'd never admit it because she never would have. She'd just lived inside her painful world, praying for someone to notice.

But no one ever did.

Even though she empathized with his pain, there was nothing she could do for him. Nothing she wanted to do. Why did she still feel this overwhelming need to try?

Since Paul's death, she hadn't noticed any man, drop-dead handsome or dirt ugly, and her unsolicited reaction disturbed her.

Why now? Why him?

Mentally shaking herself, she redirected her thoughts. She hadn't come here to ogle the local male population. Jesse Kingston interested her for two reasons and two reasons only—to find out how to contact Paul's family and to discover how much of an accident Paul's death had really been. There was no time like the present to start finding those answers.

She stood and walked to the booth where Jesse sat, his gaze still fastened on her. "Hello, Mr. Kingston. I'm Karen Ellis." She extended her hand, he ignored it. Despite the obvious snub, she waited for some reaction from Jesse, but none came. "I need to talk to you about Paul Jackson," she said before she lost her nerve.

Jesse's face grew grim and stiff. "I have nothing to say about Paul."

Throwing her what could only be classified as a disdainful glare, Jesse laid the paper aside, stood, then tossed a few bills on the table.

Deep down, Jesse knew he was being unduly harsh and absolutely unreasonable. He had no desire to discuss Paul with this woman. What he did want to do was to sweep her into his arms and obey his crazy inclination to sample her luscious lips. He shouldered past her, trying not to breath in her soft, unidentifiable perfume, and headed for the door to the diner.

Chapter 2

Jesse sat in his SUV outside his youngest half-sister Emily's house, his mind focused on Karen Ellis. The woman's beauty had stirred to life emotions that he hadn't felt in a very long time, if ever. But there were too many unanswered questions about her, and he couldn't allow his testosterone to rule his thinking.

What did she want to know about Paul and why? Had she heard about the suspicious circumstances of Paul's death? Was she one of the relatives that Paul refused to talk about, or just a nosey reporter? Though this parade of questions drummed at his mind, he knew he had other fish to fry right at the moment.

He stared at the sprawling, white, Victorian house he'd grown up in, debating on whether or not to go in. Some pretty potent memories awaited him inside that door. Was he strong enough to come face to face with them? Did he even want to?

Still groping for an answer, he glanced up in time to see the front door fly open and his half-sister Emily hurry onto the porch. Following her were Iris, Emily's mother-in-law, who had been the Kingston's housekeeper for years; Emily's husband, Kat Madison; and their twin little girls, Cat and Casey. Kat slid his free arm around Emily and pulled her close to his side.

The family picture created the same hollow ache inside Jesse that he'd felt all his life—a part of the household, but not the family.

A tap on his side window drew his attention. He turned to find his other half-sister, Diane Logan, staring in at him, a wide smile curving her lips.

"Are you planning on getting out sometime soon? Em has to put the twins to bed before dawn, you know." A wide smile softened Diane's words.

Jesse grinned sheepishly, opened the door, and stepped out. Before he knew what was happening, her welcoming arms enveloped him. Quickly, he pried himself from her embrace and took a step to the side, the small distance between them doing little to ease the discomfort he'd derived from the emotional welcome.

"How are you, Diane?" He shoved his hands in his pockets.

She stood back, then glanced over her shoulder at a man Jesse hadn't noticed before, her husband, Lou Logan. "I'm happy, Jesse, very happy." Her radiant smile affirmed it. Finally, that was one part of his past he could put to rest. If only it would all prove to be that easy.

Jesse shook hands with his newest brother-in-law. "Lou."

"Jesse. Good to have you home."

Diane reached for a young boy standing near her and pulled him to her side. "Danny, say hello to your uncle."

The boy looked exactly like his father. Danny held out his hand to Jesse. "Hi, Uncle Jesse."

"Hey, Danny." Jesse shook the small hand.

"Hey, remember us?" Emily called from the porch.

"Would you let us forget?" Diane called back, displaying the usual banter that had been the signature of his half-sisters' relationship all their lives, a relationship from which Jesse had always felt excluded.

They all headed for the porch and more hellos. By the time they were ready to go inside, Jesse still hadn't been able to shake the strange discomfort he'd gotten from their affluent greetings and his inability to return it. Coming into their lives at the age of nine, he'd never been really close to either of his half-sisters.

Hesitantly, he let Iris lead him inside the house. He paused for just a moment on the threshold. Emily's mother-in-law smiled, patted his arm and urged him forward with a gentle nudge to his back.

"It's not the same place, Jesse," Iris told him softly, then added an understanding smile.

The house was nothing like what he remembered during the time Iris had cooked and cleaned for his father. Emily had completely redecorated it with bright colors, ruffled curtains, and tons of greenery. Two identical playpens filled with toys and stuffed animals occupied the space where his father's recliner, the chair Jesse had always referred to as *the throne*, had stood. A Golden Retriever lazed in a puddle of sunlight near the playpens.

But one thing was missing that made the most distinct difference, something he'd always associated with this room—his father's cigarette smoke. This had been the room where Jesse had been forced to face his father for the first time, where he'd come to have frequent punishments meted out, where he'd confronted his father over Diane's impending, disastrous marriage to Stan, her first husband, and where he'd seen his father for the last time. The absence of the smoke that labeled the room as Frank Kingston's, more than anything else, erased his presence from the house.

"Dawg!" One of the twin girls shouted and pointed, yanking Jesse from the past.

As if on cue, the Golden Retriever stood, stretched and sauntered over to Jesse, then offered her ears to be scratched. As he obliged, he glanced at his family.

They have it all.

And what did he have? The house next door. A house he hadn't been inside of since long before he'd bought it on a whim to allow Emily to have this one, a family whose love and affection made him want to run, and enough guilt sitting on his shoulders to sink a battleship. Quite a summation of a man's life.

"Uncle Jesse?"

He roused himself, and looked down at his nephew. "Yes, Danny?"

"We're having a welcome home barbeque for you tomorrow. Mom says so." The boy made the declaration as if Diane's word ranked right up there with the Pope's.

Jesse looked at Diane, who smiled from her place at Lou's side. Jesse didn't have the heart to tell her that a family reunion wasn't high on his to-do list. All he wanted was some time alone to come to terms with the mystery of his best friend's death.

An uncomfortable laugh issued from him, then he sobered and cleared his throat of a surprising surge of emotion. "You guys don't have to do that."

Emily came forward and touched his arm. "We wanted to. We missed you." Then, as if realizing she was causing him discomfort, she stepped back, and lightened her tone.

Jesse felt another nudge to his side. Again, it was Danny. "Mom says maybe you can even bring a date, if you want."

Jesse's thoughts flew immediately to a pair of brilliant green eyes and hair the color of buttercups at twilight. In a very strange way, the image surprised him by easing the tension from his coiled nerves. But it didn't make the idea of spending an entire day as the center of his family's attention any easier to swallow.

His expression must have telegraphed his hesitation, and Kat caught it.

"Your sisters have worked all week preparing your favorite foods, so don't think you can hide out there in the woods." Kat gestured toward the thick forest bordering the back lawn where Jesse had taken refuge as a child. "Old Goldie's got a nose like a bloodhound and can find anyone." Kat winked at Jesse making light of the veiled warning not to disappoint his sisters.

Jesse looked around at their smiling faces, still amazed that they'd go to these lengths for him and that they even remembered what foods he liked.

"I guess I'd better show up then." Trying to make light of his hesitation, he winked at Kat. "There is one condition. Emily isn't cooking, is she?"

Emily laughed, then stepped forward and raised her small fist, as if she was going to punch him in the arm. Jesse instinctively pulled away. She dropped her hand and then shoved it in her pocket. Looking nervously at her husband, she moved into the circle of his arms. He held her loosely, while she glanced back at Jesse.

The expression on Emily's face, as though she'd run into an invisible brick wall, burned its way into Jesse's mind. Is that how his sisters saw him? Aloof. Untouchable?

The next day, as Karen maneuvered her car down Bristol's main street, she inhaled the sweet scent of the flowers blanketing the square. The hum of people hurrying down the street toward the church lent life to the otherwise peaceful morning ambiance of the small town. The sheer peace of the scene seeped into her tired body.

Having overslept and missed the eight o'clock B&B deadline for breakfast, Karen had opted for The Diner. While she'd been eating, she'd inquired of the waitress where she could locate Jesse Kingston. The waitress had told her that she was fairly new to the area and had no idea about Jesse's residence, but she did know where Jesse's sister Emily lived because she'd been there to buy one of Emily's Golden Retriever puppies for her daughter.

With Emily Kingston's address and directions lying on the passenger's seat, Karen headed toward the outskirts of town. Passing down tree-lined streets with kids scattered everywhere engaging in a variety of Sunday activities, she touched her flat stomach and allowed the contentment of the place to seep into her.

Oddly enough, with it came thoughts of Jesse Kingston. What was that bleakness she'd seen in his eyes? Why was a good-looking man like him sitting alone in the local eatery, looking lost, and sporting the hair-trigger temper of a bull in heat? And why did she care?

Obviously, from Jesse's rude behavior in the diner the day before, he was not going to be terribly forthcoming with information about Paul. But what she didn't understand was why. Why did he refuse to talk to her about his best friend? And it hadn't been just the refusal. The look on his face had almost dared her to push him, but to be ready to suffer the consequences.

Whatever his reason, she would not leave Bristol until he answered her questions. She gently caressed her tummy. "Don't worry, little one. We'll find your family. I promise."

About fifteen minutes later, she pulled into the driveway of a beautiful, old Victorian house. Several cars were parked in the driveway. Too many to belong to the small family the waitress had said Emily had. Not wanting to interrupt what looked like it might be some sort of family gathering, Karen reached for the key to restart the car and leave.

"Hi, can I help you?"

Karen started and for a moment could only stare at the blond woman peeking in her open car window. Then as if someone had jabbed her in the ribs, she roused herself.

"Hi. I'm Karen Ellis. I'm looking for Jesse Kingston, and I was told I could find someone here who could tell me where he lives. I need to talk to him on an urgent matter." She glanced around at the other vehicles. "But I don't want to interrupt your party. I can come back another time."

The strikingly lovely woman extended her hand. "I'm Diane Logan, Jesse's sister. He'll be here shortly. This is a welcome home party for him. And you're here now, so why don't you wait?"

"Oh, I don't—"

"Please," Diane said, opening the car door and beckoning for Karen to get out. "No sense in making an extra trip. Besides, if it's urgent, then you'll be wanting to see him sooner rather than later."

Karen could have kissed her. "If you're sure. I don't want to spoil your party."

"You won't spoil anything, and if you knew me better," Diane said, "you'd know I don't say anything unless I mean it. Now, let me take you around back and introduce you to the mob."

Almost unconsciously, because it had become an extension of her arm, Karen grabbed her camera from the seat and hooked the strap over her shoulder. Since she had started working on a pictorial coffee table book about rural America, she'd brought the camera along on her trip to Bristol hoping she'd get some shots of the locale after she'd spoken with Jesse.

She followed Diane across the lawn to the backyard. As they rounded the corner of the house, she came face to face with a picture that made envy rise up to choke her. Before her was the exact scenario she'd dreamed of seeing her baby a part of one day.

Two identical little girls fought over a tire swing while a man, obviously their father, refereed. In the corner of the yard, a large Golden Retriever barked merrily at a man and a young boy tossing a football back and forth while they watched over a grill wafting out mouth-watering aromas. Not far from the grill, two women were setting a picnic table for a meal.

Karen was enthralled with the family scene and turned to thank Diane for including her. Before she could say anything, Jesse's sister led Karen to the picnic table and within minutes had introduced her to everyone. To Karen's astonishment, they all treated her like a member of the family and not a party crasher, even though that's how she saw herself.

Karen adjusted her seat at the wooden picnic table and raised her camera. Focusing, she snapped a picture of Emily's twin girls pouring sand into each other's hair in the sandbox. She had just clicked the shutter, when their mother discovered them and hauled them both off toward the hose on the side of the house. Once she got Emily and Kat to sign one of the release forms she had in the car, the photo would make a great cover shot for her book.

Karen had been working on the book for months and already had a sizable advance in her bank account to help her get through the baby's birth and the time after. Now, if she could just find the enthusiasm to finish it. Since Paul's death, her instincts for survival made her focus all her attention and energies on her baby and its well-being.

Watching this close, loving family interact made her that much more determined to find Paul's family so her baby could have this kind of support, love, and closeness, a wonderful addition to the love she knew the child would get from her grandfather and her Aunt Elle.

"Ah ha, we have a shutterbug among us," Emily announced,

flopping down beside Karen and eyeing the camera and its bulky zoom lens. "The expertise with which you handle that complicated looking thing makes me think this is more than just a hobby."

Karen laughed and laid the camera on the picnic table. "Guilty. I'm a freelance photographer."

Before she could say more, something over Karen's shoulder drew Emily's attention. Jesse's sister smiled in the direction of the field beyond the lawn's edge and stood, their conversation forgotten. "Do my eyes deceive me or is our brother deigning to join us?"

Everyone, including Karen, turned their attention toward the man coming toward them. Jesse Kingston, his measured gate marked with obvious reluctance, slowly made his way through the field's high grass, his head bent, as if studying each step, his dark hair glistening in the sunlight.

By the time he'd reached them, Diane had come to stand next to Karen. Jesse's older sister laid her hand on Karen's arm and announced, "Karen Ellis, I assume you know my brother, Jesse."

Jesse looked Karen in the eye and nodded curtly. Even though his greeting was less than cordial, Karen's insides twisted with a strange pleasure. When his simmering, dark gaze touched her, a bottomless sensation invaded her stomach. An inexplicable warmth swept through her body. She grappled for a reason for the unexpected emotions rushing through her. It had to be pregnancy hormones. Determined not to let him get to her on any level, personal or otherwise, she centered her gaze on his face. What she saw there didn't surprise her. There it was again, that stark loneliness.

Jesse hid any spark of surprise at finding Karen here with his family. "Yes, Ms. Ellis and I have met." He'd made every excuse to himself not to come here and failed to find anything that he thought his family would accept. Now, seeing this woman again, the woman who had insinuated herself into his dreams last night, he wished he'd tried harder.

Diane looked at Karen, questions evident in her expression. "But . . . ."

"Your brother and I met at The Diner." She dragged her amused gaze from Jesse to Diane. "But we didn't have a chance to really talk."

Her soft voice swept over him like a breeze off his beloved mountains. The woman hadn't lost an ounce of appeal. And he hadn't become less reactive to it. He rubbed his palms together to remove the light sheen of perspiration that had broken out there.

"Pleasure meeting you . . . again, Ms. Ellis." He dipped his head just enough to move his gaze from her face to her breasts. The lack of a bra was evidence by the small, turgid peaks pressing against the material of her blouse. His groin stirred to life. Quickly, he glanced away, then checked out the activity in the yard. "Looks like everyone's here."

"We've just been waiting for you," Diane said, eyeing him with a look that said *we were afraid you wouldn't show.*

"Then let the festivities begin."

Diane laughed. "I hate to point this out, little brother, but the festivities are well under way already. It's the food that's been waiting. Iris will be relieved that her picnic lunch hasn't been ruined. Excuse me, Karen." Diane hurried toward the back door of the house.

Jesse grabbed a cold beer from the galvanized tub holding the iced drinks, then ignoring Karen, he strolled to the seclusion of a large oak tree at the side of the yard and sat in the dark circle of its shade. From there, he could watch his family playing games and interacting.

But he didn't stay centered on them for long. Instead, he found his gaze drawn to Karen. Who was she, and what did she want? Why had Diane invited a stranger to join in a family event? From the corner of his eye, he caught Karen studying him. Then, to his displeasure, she started to walk in his direction. Evidently, the woman didn't understand the meaning of *I don't want to talk to you.*

She'd only gone a few steps, when she raised her camera, then snapped a picture of him.

"What's that for?" he asked, when she got close enough.

"Posterity." She sat beside him.

Her perfume wafted to him on the light breeze that picked up a few strands of her hair and then laid them on her cheek. He itched to brush them away, test the feel of her skin, but fisted his hand around the cold beer can and asked the question that had popped into his head the moment he recognized her "Why are you here? Certainly not to snap pictures of a family you don't even know."

Karen stared off into the woods beyond the lawn. By the time she spoke again, he'd all but decided she wasn't going to answer him.

"The pictures are for a coffee table book I'm putting together. And I'm here because Diane asked me to stay so I could speak with you." She turned to him, her face serious, her bottom lip quivering ever so slightly. "I was Paul Jackson's girlfriend, and I have some questions to ask you about him."

Girlfriend?

The word exploded inside Jesse's head like a firecracker. How could she have been Paul's girlfriend?

Paul was married.

Chapter 3

How could this woman be Paul's girlfriend when he was already married? Before Jesse could ask, Diane and Emily walked across the freshly mowed backyard and sat beside him and Karen beneath the old oak's spreading limbs.

"Iris will be bringing out the food in a few minutes," Diane announced, then turned to Jesse. "Karen needs a picture of some of the sites around town. Em and I figured you could show them to her. Maybe take her up to the ice caves." His matchmaking sisters' smiles reflected a small degree of self-satisfaction and the bright glow of manipulation.

They both knew that the caves were miles from any civilization, infrequently visited by anyone, even tourists, and the perfect place for two people who wanted to be alone. Problem was, being alone with a woman who played on his emotions like an expert violinist played a Stradivarius was the last thing he wanted.

Before either Karen or Jesse could comment on his sister's suggestion, Iris called everyone to gather around and help themselves to a platter piled high with barbequed chicken, a bowl of potato salad and a rectangular pan of baked beans. The four of them rose and slowly made their way across the yard.

For the next hour, all conversation halted as everyone dug in. Jesse had missed Iris's cooking. Shortly after the main course had disappeared and the bowls and platter stood empty, Iris disappeared inside the house. Smiling, she emerged through the screen door carrying a scrumptious-looking chocolate cake. She set it carefully on the picnic table and then picked up a serving knife.

"I don't suppose anyone wants any of this." Iris grinned at her twin granddaughters, who whooped and scampered to her side.

"Me do," one of the girls demanded, tugging on Iris's apron hem.

"Me some," the other one chimed in.

Emily groaned and levered herself from the picnic table bench beside Karen. "I couldn't wait until they could walk and talk, but I'm beginning to think temporary insanity drove me to wish for such things." She sighed and helped Iris cut small pieces for each of the girls. "I'm glad they've at least gotten teeth and aren't eating that disgusting mush anymore. Now, if we could only conquer potty training."

Laughter rippled over the group.

Iris patted her daughter-in-law's hand. "All in good time. All in good time."

"Hey, Jesse, have some cake. My mother makes the best chocolate cake you have ever put in your mouth." Kat kissed Iris's cheek and smiled down at her with a cherishing grin.

Jesse glanced at mother and son. It was hard to believe they'd only just been reunited after being separated most of Kat's life. It certainly didn't resemble the reunion that had taken place in this house when, at age nine and with a newly deceased mother, Jesse had come here to live and met his father and sisters for the first time.

Jesse forced a smile. "It's a good thing someone in your family can cook, or you'd starve to death." He looked pointedly at Emily.

"Now, that's not true. Iris is not the only cook in the family." Emily paused in the task of wiping chocolate frosting from her daughter's face, then grinned up at her handsome husband. "Kat makes a really mean lasagna." She looked at Diane, who gave her a thumbs-up, then at her brother. "And I'd appreciate it, Jesse Kingston, if you would find a topic of conversation other than my lousy cooking."

"But you're so cute when you're defending yourself," he teased back.

Karen glanced at Jesse. *Verbal banter. Safe. No emotional commitment. No physical contact allowed.*

She knew how that worked. She'd often seen Paul do it. If you sidetracked people long enough with inanities, they didn't dig for the real answers. Jesse's silence added one more missing piece to the puzzle that made up this man. She swept her mind clear of any need to finish this particular puzzle. She had no desire to get involved in any small way with another man who was unwilling to share himself.

The family crowded around the picnic table for desert, and Karen noted that Jesse positioned himself at the very end of the bench, away from the core of activity.

When one of Emily's girls sidled up to him, he offered her some of his cake. Her sister, not to be done out of her share of Uncle Jesse's dessert, quickly joined them.

He leaned back and studied them. "How do you tell them apart, Em?"

Karen stepped in. "It's easy." She turned to Emily. "May I enlighten your brother?"

Emily nodded. "Sure. Someone needs to tell him the secret. After all, they're his nieces, and he can't go on forever calling them *Hey You*."

"Cat has a brown mole on her right wrist." Karen watched as Jesse checked it out, then smiled when he proved her right. "Casey doesn't have one."

"I Cat," the little girl announced, holding up the wrong arm for proof of her identity in an attempt to relieve any doubt as to which identical twin was which.

The twin's father frowned at Karen. "How did you know?'

"I take pictures for a living and I'm really tuned in to small details. Besides, Cat explained it to me shortly after I got here."

Everyone laughed.

It suddenly struck Karen how odd it was that a stranger had learned the secret of how to tell the difference between his nieces and their own uncle hadn't. What a strange man.

Detecting a slight softening of her attitude toward Paul's friend, Karen redirected her thoughts. Jesse Kingston may hold himself aloof from the rest of the world, but he hadn't tangled with Karen's determination yet. She needed information and whether Jesse liked it or not, she would pry it out of him if it was the last thing she ever did. But so far his family had unintentionally shielded him from any questions she might have.

However, his family would not always be around for him to hide behind.

Jesse eased the SUV around a pothole in Emily's driveway. He checked for oncoming traffic, then swung the car onto the main road that would take them back to Bristol. Thanks to Diane backing him into a corner, when Karen's car had refused to start Jesse had been delegated to drive her back to the bed and breakfast. Short of being rude, he could do nothing except acquiesce.

With Emily's promise to have Kat look at the car first thing in the morning, then bring it to the bed and breakfast still ringing in their ears, they were now sitting in the front seat of Jesse's car like two wooden soldiers, neither of them able to find words to start a conversation.

"You didn't have to do this, you know." Karen's voice filled the car's muggy interior.

"And how would you have gotten back to town?" Jesse opened the vents on the AC, adjusted the temperature, then hit the switch to turn on the fan.

"I'm sure I'd have found a way." She paused. "Kat could have taken me."

"Kat was putting the twins to bed." Considering Jesse had tried his best to get out of driving her, he was surprised at feeling a little put out that she didn't want to be here any more than he did and that the thought of her being, even innocently, with another man bothered him—a lot. Rather than dwell on that, he asked her something else that had been bothering him. "How did you know?"

Karen turned to him, her striking beauty illuminated by the dash lights. "How did I know what?"

"About the mole. Which twin was which."

She threw her head back and laughed. The sound washed the tension of the day from him or maybe it was the absence of the pressure he always felt around his family. His grip on the steering wheel relaxed.

"I told you how. Cat told me."

"But—"

"She may not talk well, but she can certainly make herself understood when it comes down to who's going to take the next turn on the swing." Karen shifted in the seat to face him. Her bent knee brushed his thigh, sending funny little prickles zipping down his leg. "When I took them to the swing, Emily said to allow Cat to go first because they made it a rule that they had to take turns. Casey had gone first last time. When we got there, I couldn't figure out who was who. Cat enlightened me by telling me her name and showing me the mole."

Out of the corner of his eye, he could see Karen studying him. "I think that's called cheating." He cast a quick look in her direction, then returned his gaze to the safer path of the car's headlights on the darkened road.

"If you'd made time to play with them, you'd have found it out, too," she said softly.

The statement slashed a pain through his insides. It wasn't that he didn't want to get closer to his family. He just knew that when you get too close to anything, fate finds a way to drive you apart again. He'd tried for years to get close to his father and in the end, the pain of not being able to drove a wedge between them, and he'd lost not only his father, but his family as well.

Having had enough of family for one day, he shook his head. "About the sights around town . . . ."

"Please don't feel that you have to take me. I'll find them on my own. I'm sure someone in town can direct me." Karen couldn't believe she was throwing away a golden opportunity to be alone with Jesse and finally get to talk to him about Paul. She only knew that she was more aware of him now than she'd ever been of any man in her life. She needed time to come to terms with that before jumping into a situation where there would be no one but them around.

"I'm glad you said that. I don't think it would be a good move either."

Well, he'd jumped at that like a fish to a worm, she thought, insanely regretting she'd made it so easy for him to back out.

Having nothing to add, Karen leaned her head back against the seat. The quiet and the motion of the car lulled her into a half sleep. All that fresh air and exercise she'd had today, plus not sleeping well in a strange bed, were taking their toll. She'd missed her shower the evening before and ended up having to set her alarm for seven to get into the bathroom before any of the other guests, but had still managed to miss breakfast.

"So, how did you like the Kingston family's version of a backyard barbecue?"

Karen yawned, then stretched. "Well, in addition to having one of the best days I can ever remember, I got a terrific taste of rural life. For instance, I know now that I can find room for chocolate cake, even when I'm sure my stomach can't hold another ounce of food. I also know that after the sun goes down the human body becomes a target for every blood-sucking insect in the world." She absently itched one of the insect bites on the fair skin of her inner arm.

Her profile drew his gaze. With her hair tousled by the breeze coming from the AC vent and a trace of sunburn coloring her cheeks, she took his breath away. He didn't think anything could surpass the beauty he found in his mountains, but Karen did. And it wasn't just surface beauty. Quickly, he averted his attention back to the road.

Despite his best efforts not to, he recalled how she'd interacted with the twins, and how he'd envied her relaxed ease with them and Danny. She'd fit in with his family like an old comfortable shoe, something he'd always longed for, but was never been able to achieve and then shied away from all together. Karen had done it in one short afternoon without even trying and had soaked every second up like a thirsty sponge. She had an ability to draw people to her like flies to honey, an inner beauty that radiated . . . what?

He had no idea. But whatever it was, Jesse knew that particular quality had been missing from his makeup for as long as he could remember. He just didn't mix with people. Which is why he was better suited to the solitude of the forest. But even that had been marred now by Paul's death.

Thoughts of Paul reminded him that he had no business thinking about Karen like any other woman. She wasn't any other woman. She'd been Paul's girlfriend. Paul's *illicit* girlfriend, he reminded himself. Had she known Paul was married? No. After having seen her genuineness today, he could not believe she would intentionally step between a man and his family.

Jesse pulled the SUV to the curb in front of The Land of Nod Bed and Breakfast and stopped.

"Jesse, I want to ask you something, and it may not be any of my business, but . . . ." Karen paused and stared out the window.

"But?" He held his breath waiting for her to ask about Paul.

When she turned her face to him, shadows made it impossible for him to see her expression. "Why do you hold your family at arm's length? I mean they're so warm and friendly, and you just don't seem to even try to fit in. I never really had a family like that and . . . well, I'd have given just about anything to have had all those loving people around me all the time. "

That was definitely not what Jesse had expected. Relief took hold of him first, followed quickly by surprise, then a wave of anger at the imposition of her prying into his personal life. A product of long conditioning, his defenses rose like an invisible shield against a towering beast. "You're right. It's none of your business."

She sighed and released the seat belt. Turning to him, she laid a hand on his thigh. "They want you to be part of them, part of their lives. Can't you see that?"

Easy for her to say. His family may want him to join in now, but what about later? What about when they found out what had happened that day in the woods? How did he live with the pain of their rejection again?

He removed her hand where it burned into his flesh through the fabric of his jeans and sent strange sensations through him, tempting him to do things they'd both be sorry for come morning, forcing him to remember how very much he wanted to kiss her. "Leave it alone, Karen. It's almost eleven o'clock. You should be going inside and getting some sleep."

She pursed her lips stubbornly.

Jesse's breath caught in his throat. What did those lips taste like? Were they soft, warm, moist?

"I can't leave it alone," she said. "I guess it's the nurturer in me. Or maybe it's just that I always wanted what you seem to push away every chance you get. I guess I don't understand why I see you hurting and them trying to ease that hurt, and you just won't let them."

His anger built, unreasonable fueling his need to kiss her. "Stay out of it," he ground out.

She opened her mouth to speak again. He could think of only one way to silence her. The one thing that had taken over every sane thought in his head. He grabbed her, hauled her into his arms, then covered her lips with his.

At first he tried to punish her for interfering in his life, for resurrecting Paul, for making him want things he couldn't have. But then, when her lips relaxed under his, and she showed no sign of struggle, the kiss changed. Subtly at first, then deepening by degrees. He relaxed his mouth and sent his tongue to explore the shape of her lips. Slowly, he outlined them, tasted their sweetness, learning their texture.

Then she opened her mouth to him like a baby bird waiting for sustenance. Accepting her silent invitation, his tongue snaked between her teeth. She groaned softly, and he pulled her closer, aligning her curves with the hard surface of his body.

Suddenly, she pushed him away. The handle on the driver's door dug into his spine. Struggling to find his center of gravity, he took in large gulps of night air.

"This . . . is . . . wrong," she said, her breathing erratic, her hair tangled invitingly around her face. She brushed it away from her eyes, then breathed deep. "We have to think about . . . Paul."

Think about Paul? Hell, he'd thought of little else since the wildfire.

But before he could voice his thoughts, she'd jumped from the car, hurried up the hedge-lined walk, then disappeared into the house.

For a long time, Jesse sat there staring at the house, trying to get his emotions back in line. He couldn't let this happen, this . . . whatever it was about this woman that drew him like a moth to a flame. Unlike the moth, in the end he'd wind up with more than singed wings. Karen still had strong feelings for Paul. He could hear it in her voice when she said his name. And, no matter how right it had felt, kissing her could only mean trouble, and more trouble was the very last thing he needed right now.

After a few minutes had passed, he saw the light in a second story window come on. The curtain was pulled aside and someone peered out. Quickly, the figure stepped back, then pulled the shade. That simple act made Jesse feel he'd just been cut out of some else's life.

All the way home, Jesse relived the kiss he'd shared with Karen. That common sense had prevailed pleased him. That she had taken the initiative and ended the kiss bothered the hell out of him. Hindsight is 20/20, but he should have been the one to pull back, not Karen. Far from a novice with women, he'd never experienced anything to equal that kiss before in his life. It had shaken him right down to the soles of his feet, and, while he'd initiated it, she'd been as much a participant as he had—until thoughts of Paul stopped her. It annoyed him that she had even wanted to end it.

However, the effect it had and continued to have on him bothered him even more. The memory of how her mouth had felt beneath his occupied his thoughts, overriding the warning bells going off in his head, and most of all, making him wish for things that could never be. He kept recalling how her laughter spread warmth through him, how her smile lit up her whole face, the way her touch made his skin tingle for more, the way she fit into his family better than he ever had. Without even trying, Karen had become a part of him.

Was the woman a witch? Had she woven a spell that had them all captured in her silky web?

No more, he told himself. *It can't happen again.* Once was an accident. Twice would be emotional suicide. Aside from her connection to Paul, getting involved with a woman from the city had to be one of the stupidest things he'd ever contemplated.

Hadn't his father's experience with his mother taught him anything? Sure, Karen would be happy now, when country life was all new and exciting, but what about after the shine wore off? What then? She'd be back in her little red sports car, speeding toward New York, back to the place that spelled safety and comfort for her. And where would he be? Would he turn into a bitter, resentful old man like his father?

No. He refused to spend his life like Frank Kingston had—making other people pay for his disappointments and his mistakes. But, despite all his arguments and common sense analogies, the fact remained that Jesse could not get Karen off his mind.

Besides, it was all a moot point anyway. He couldn't get involved with the girlfriend of the man he'd allowed to die. But did he have to let it go that far? He was an adult, after all, not some adolescent with out-of-control hormones. All he had to do was remove the temptation.

Couldn't he just keep her at arm's length, control his own emotions, tell her what she wanted to know about Paul, help her get her pictures as quickly as possible, then encourage her to leave town? He realized that it was little compensation for a life, and that nothing would ever replace Paul, but could Jesse *not* help her?

Still fully clothed, Karen lay across her bed. What in God's name had she been thinking to let him kiss her? Letting him wasn't the half of it, she corrected. How could she have responded like a twenty-dollar wanton to a man she'd just met?

But worst of all, why hadn't she talked to him about Paul? She couldn't have asked for a better opportunity. Yet, she hadn't taken advantage of it. When the answer—an answer she didn't like at all—occurred to her, she realized it was because Jesse had pushed away all thoughts of her baby's father.

She lay there for a long time, thinking about it. What was the attraction she felt for Jesse? And why was it strong enough to veer her away from her intended path? She waited, but no answers came.

Added to that, she didn't even know why she'd started the conversation about his acceptance of his family. He'd been totally right. She'd stuck her nose in where it didn't belong. She'd get her answers about the fire and Paul's family, then she'd be gone, and life in the sleepy little hamlet of Bristol would go on. How it went on was none of her concern.

When would she learn that there were some things that were better left alone? Like men with some big-time emotional problems, and dark cars that invited intimacy with a man she had no business even thinking about, much less kissing him as if her life depended on it. Let the Kingstons exorcize their family ghosts. She had her own problems to contend with.

Resolutely, she jumped up, then went to the dresser where she extracted her nightie from the top drawer. Throwing it, her towel, and a robe over her arm, she headed down the hall to the shared bathroom. Her bedside clock had read eleven o'clock. She still had a half hour before her landlady turned off the hot water. Putting thoughts of Jesse and their encounter aside, she concentrated on enjoying a relaxing shower and then a good night's sleep.

Laying her nightie on the vanity and hanging her robe on the back of the door and the towel over the bar, she moved aside a shower curtain covered with all species of colorful tropical fish and resembled the inside of a giant aquarium. She adjusted the water to the hot temperature she preferred, then stripped off her clothes and stepped under the spray.

The silky caress of the water brought to mind again the feel of Jesse's lips on hers, the way he gently stroked her mouth, almost as if he worshiped it. Her body began to tingle anew and not from the hot water. Slowly, she ran her hands over her skin, her mind conjuring up the image of a man, but not just any man. *Jesse Kingston.*

Taking the soap, she lathered her body, then massaged the bubbles into her sensitive skin. Slipping back beneath the spray, she leaned against the tiled side of the shower stall. Eyes closed, she luxuriated in the sensual feel of the hot water running over her, rinsing away the velvet lather like a lover's hands easing away the sweet ache of desire. *Jesse's hands.*

Down deep, she knew with a certainty that making love with Jesse Kingston would be an experience she'd never recover from. Right now, even with her skin tingling and her lips still swollen from their kiss, she wasn't willing to take that risk.

Tiny shards of ice attacked her without warning. Her eyes flew open. She'd stood under the shower much longer than she'd intended. The water had turned to arctic runoff. Her memory played back Mildred Hopkins' warning. The diminutive landlady had been quite firm.

I turn off the water heater at eleven-thirty. No sense letting it run all night. That's just a waste of good money.

Gasping for breath and fighting a shower curtain that insisted on adhering itself to her slick body, Karen battled her way out of the shower. Grabbing her thick bath towel from the towel bar, she wrapped it around her frigid body, tuned off the water, then leaned against the sink, gasping for air.

Talk about your rude awakenings. *I'll have to remember this for the next time I have a run-in with Jesse.* No, there would be no more run-ins, no more incidents of her sticking her nose in where it didn't belong. And above all, no more kisses.

Jesse posed far too much danger to her peace of mind, and she'd do well to remember that. She had not come here to have an affair with a man who could leave scars the size of Texas on her heart, a man who carried his own scars and refuse to share them with anyone. She may know way more than she wanted about the Kingston family and nothing about the brother who held himself apart, but she didn't plan on rectifying that. The less she knew, the better. Once she'd learned what she needed to know, she'd head back to the safety of New York City.

Grabbing her nightclothes and slipping them on, she headed back to her room. So much for a good night's sleep. She deposited her dirty clothes in a pile beside the dresser, promising herself she'd pick them up in the morning. Throwing her head forward, she began towel drying her hair. The vigorous massage felt good and helped her vanquish thoughts of Jesse from her mind.

A knock at the door stopped her. She sighed. The last thing she needed at midnight was a heart-to-heart with her landlady. Couldn't the woman tell time? The knock came again, this time more insistent. It didn't look like she was going to give up. Karen figured she might as well answer it.

Realizing she'd left her robe in the bathroom, she held the towel in front of her, strode to the door, then threw it open.

"Mildred, it's—"

Mouth agape, Karen went numb. Her fingers relaxed their grip on the towel. It slithered down her body to the floor. Unable to move, she knew that nothing but a thin covering of revealing, peach silk and lace hid her nakedness from the mesmerized gaze of Jesse Kingston.

Chapter 4

When Jesse climbed back into his car, he was still reeling from his encounter with Karen.

He had no idea exactly what he'd said, just that he'd babbled about changing his mind and, if she still wanted a tour of the local sites, he'd meet her at The Diner the next morning. He wasn't even sure she'd answered him. Beyond that, all he could remember was dashing out of the house with the tantalizing image of Karen in that skimpy nightie with her creamy skin and those dark circles in the center of each plump breast peeking through the lace.

Rubbing his eyes as if he could erase her image, he sighed and then stared sightlessly out the windshield. What the hell was wrong with him? She wasn't the first beautiful woman he'd ever encountered.

Resolutely, he wiped beads of sweat from his forehead, adjusted his aroused lower body to a more comfortable position and started the car. If he didn't get his testosterone under control, this woman would be his death or what he really feared was she might become his life.

For a long time after Jesse hurried away, Karen remained frozen in place. While she fought to gain control of her breathing, she envisioned the look on Jesse's face, one she'd never seen on Paul's in all the time they were together. It was more than raw sexual attraction. But she couldn't put her finger on exactly what it was that had affected her so powerfully.

In that moment, when she'd opened the door and Jesse had taken in the sight of her near nudity, something had happened between them, something she knew in her gut would complicate what was supposed to be a simple fact-finding trip. Was it possible that it was just the normal reaction of two healthy people coming face to face with an embarrassing moment? Or was it something even more dangerous?

Slowly, she closed the door, flipped off the lights, and then, skin still tingling from Jesse's blatant appraisal of her body, climbed into bed, certain that this would be a very, very long night.

The next morning The Diner was overflowing with early patrons. All of them, much to Jesse's chagrin, were too interested in the Kingston boy and the city girl. Mostly the city girl.

"Hey, Jesse, who's your friend?"

Jesse looked up to see Fred Connors, the middle-aged owner of the local drugstore, grinning at Karen. The twinkle of intense interest lighting Fred's gray eyes sent an irrational spike of jealousy through Jesse. Fred had a perfect right to be interested in Karen. Jesse had no claim on her, nor did he want one. But that rationalization didn't cool Jesse's boiling blood.

He glanced past Fred to the counter. "I see your breakfast has been served up." He leveled a challenging glare at Fred. "Wouldn't want it to get cold, would you?"

Fred turned a deep shade of crimson and backed up. "Uh, no. Nothing worse than cold eggs," he said. "No offense, Jesse." Fred hurried away.

"None taken, Fred." Without looking at the man, Jesse cut a hunk from the fried egg on the plate in front of him.

Karen frowned at him. "Was that necessary? He was just being friendly. After all, I'm a stranger in town, and he probably wondered who I am. Wouldn't it have been more polite to simply introduce me?"

Refraining from pointing out that being friendly was most probably not what the man had in mind, Jesse propped his fork on the edge of his plate, steepled his hands in front of him and looked Karen in the eyes. "When you've lived in a small town as long as I have, you learn that every breath you take is reported up and down

Main Street with the speed of light. The less you tell them, the less they talk."

Karen grinned. "But isn't that just whetting their appetite for speculation?"

She was right. He knew that nothing got the gossip mill's wheels turning faster than a mystery. If they didn't get answers, they created their own. Still, something in him selfishly stopped him from sharing Karen with anyone, yet, and most especially another man. Why, he wasn't sure, nor was he ready to explore the reasons.

Shrugging, Jesse picked up his coffee cup and took a long swallow, then set the cup back in the saucer. It had barely been replaced when the waitress appeared carrying a steaming carafe.

"Refill?"

Feeling the waitress's inquisitive eyes boring into him then Karen, Jesse glanced at Karen's empty plate. He'd had enough of them being the centerpiece of the town's morning amusement. "No thanks. We're done." He rose. "Let's get out of here." He threw some bills on the table and stood aside for Karen to precede him.

In the car, she swung sideways in the seat to face Jesse. "Want to tell me what that was all about?"

"No," he said and started the car. A moment later they were moving down Main Street. "So where to? The ice caves?"

For a long time Karen just stared at his set profile. "No," she said with as much determination as he'd just shown. "I want to go to the woods and see where Paul died in the fire."

Jesse's jaw tightened. He pulled the car to the roadside. Leaving the engine idling, he turned to her. He had no idea why, but he was suddenly overwhelmed by a need to protect her. "Why would you want to go there?"

Karen clasped her hands tightly in her lap and stared at them. "I don't know. I never had a chance to pay my last respects. Maybe I just need a place to grieve." She raised her gaze to Jesse. "Maybe it'll bring closure. Maybe not. I just know I need to go there."

Though everything in him told him this was not a smart move, he couldn't help but respond to her emotional reply. Finally, he nodded and pulled the car back onto the highway. For nearly an hour they rode without conversing, each deep in their own thoughts.

Finally, when she could stand the silence no longer, Karen ventured a question. "How well did you know Paul?"

When Jesse didn't answer right away, Karen was certain this was going to be another of those questions Jesse met with a wall of stony silence. When he did answer, it surprised her.

"I thought I knew him quite well. But—"

"But what?"

"Let's just say he wasn't big on sharing his personal life."

Evidently, Paul hadn't been any more open with Jesse than he'd been with her. At this rate, she'd never find out about Paul's family and her baby would end up never knowing them. But she wouldn't give up that easily.

Not wanting Jesse to retreat back into his *I'm-not-answering-that* mode, she worked to make the next questions sound nonchalant. "And professionally?"

He frowned. "Professionally? I knew him well enough to wonder why he'd—" He stopped abruptly, threw her a glance and then centered his attention back on his driving. His hands tightened on the steering wheel.

Did Jesse have doubts about Paul's death too? She shifted in the seat to face him squarely and pressed for an answer. "Wonder why he'd what?"

"You know, Karen, there were three main reasons I became a forest ranger and decided to live in the woods: Mother Nature doesn't reject her children, and the trees and animals don't ask questions."

Pushing aside his underlying sarcasm, Karen couldn't help but concentrate on the reference to Mother Nature not rejecting her children. Had Jesse been rejected? Certainly not by his family. Maybe by his father? Knowing that same rejection, her heart went out to him. She wanted to touch him, to console him in some way, but a gut feeling told her any compassion she could offer would be met with that wall of silent anger that he'd shown her so many times.

Instead, she asked the obvious. "And the third reason?"

His lips tightened into a set line. "We're here," he said, pulling the car to stop beside the road.

She could almost hear the door slam on his answer. Well, he hadn't won yet. They had the rest of the day, and Jesse Kingston had no idea how relentless she could be when she wanted information. What she didn't understand was why it was so important that she know, why was she so concerned with his state of mind?

Karen walked the tree line around the spot where Jesse said they'd found Paul's body. Unless she got some answers, this was the closest she'd ever come to visiting his grave site.

Blackened stumps dotted the scorched earth, along with the charred remains of burned leaves and grass. It didn't take an expert eye to see that the fire that had rampaged through here had done so at an astoundingly high temperature. The unmistakable odor of burned wood still hung in the air.

Here and there, spots of green peeked through the carnage, a sign that Mother Nature had already started to reclaim the forest. It would take years, but eventually, this entire area would bear no signs that a man had lost his life here.

A few yards away, beyond the fire damage, Karen spotted a whitish rock. She picked it up and placed it in the middle of the blackened area. Tears burned at the back of her eyes. Placing her hand over her stomach, she said a silent goodbye to her friend.

Friend?

That thought surprised her. Paul had been a man she'd loved, a man with whom she'd been intimate and created a child, a man with whom she'd been ready to plan a future. Why then was she thinking of him as merely a friend?

Seemingly of its own volition, her gaze moved to Jesse. Was

he the reason? Paul had been her lover and her friend, but was Jesse her destiny?

Jesse had been watching Karen as she moved about the burn site. What was she thinking? Was her heart breaking? He had to fight the urge to cradle her close and tell her the pain would go away. But would it?

He'd been trying to erase it for months. Despite his efforts, it seemed as sharp and bitter as it had the day Paul had ordered Jesse to stand clear and left him to watch as his superior walked into a burning forest, knowing in his heart that the chances of Paul coming out alive were slim.

Unreasonable anger at Paul's carelessness churned inside Jesse. If only he'd said to hell with their rank and had forced Paul to listen to him. If only he'd made Paul see sense. If only he knew why Paul had ordered him to stay behind in the first place. So many unanswered questions.

He stared fixedly at the white rock Karen had placed in the middle of the burn site. The starkness of it made Jesse think about how much this place resembled him: barren, burned out, and bleak. Eventually, the carnage that had scarred the forest would disappear and new life would fill it, making it green and lush and alive. Could he ever hope for the same for himself?

"A memorial?" He motioned toward the rock, hoping by speaking he could block out his torturing thoughts.

She nodded. "It's a small tribute, but this place needs to be marked." She sighed and looked into the branches of the skeletal, black trees above them. "I keep asking myself why Paul, a man who taught safety to new rangers, a man who had won awards for his performance in the line of duty, could have been so careless." She shook her head and turned to Jesse. "I can't find any answers. Can you? Do you have the answers, Jesse?"

He strode to where she stood in the middle of the blackened landscape. His arm brushed against her. Wanting to rub the tingles that shot through his skin, he stepped away just far enough to break the contact. "I've asked myself that a thousand times in the last few months. I'm afraid I don't have any answers for you either."

Karen's expression suddenly changed. The frustration of trying to find answers to her questions faded. Her face took on a look that could only be described as pure determination and unwavering stubbornness. "Then it's time we got some."

He looked around at the fire's ruins and frowned. Even to his trained eye, there were no clues to be found here, nothing that would tell them anything about what had happened after Paul had disappeared from sight that day. "This is going to need an expert eye."

"Yes, and neither of us has a background for it." Then she smiled, and Jesse's gut did a somersault. "But I know someone who does."

Karen moved off to the edge of the burn site. As she walked, she pulled her cell phone out of her jeans pocket and then punched in a series of numbers from memory. She carried on a muffled conversation, then closed the phone and returned it to her pocket and smiled broadly at Jesse.

"My sister Elle's an arson investigator. She's agreed to come up here from Florida and see what she can find."

On their trip down the mountain, Karen summoned the courage to ask Jesse the question that had been nagging at her. "What was the third reason you became a ranger?"

Jesse sighed. "Don't you ever stop asking questions?"

"Does a leopard change its spots?"

He glanced at her. A smirk twisted the corner of her mouth. His heart did a quick flutter. Damn, the woman had a way about her that just played havoc with his libido. But it was more than the sexual attraction this time. He saw something in her eyes foreign to him—understanding.

Suddenly it seemed important to give her an answer. "From the time I came to live with my father and my stepsisters, the forest had been a refuge for me. When things had gotten rough at home,

I'd always found peace and happiness there. When I got old enough I made it my permanent home and never regretted it—until Paul died." He glanced in her direction. "Now that you've picked my brain for all my deepest secrets, how about we take that trip to the ice caves?"

Karen didn't believe for a minute that his one statement covered all the secrets that this mysterious man held inside, but this was a start. What puzzled her, however, was that finding out more about Jesse was beginning to take on more importance than finding Paul's family.

Chapter 5

Karen was astounded at what she found after they parked the car in the area that had been fashioned into a crude parking lot, traipsed through the trees, climbed up rocky cliffs, and finally arrived at the ice caves. Though treacherous, they were all Jesse's sister had said they'd be. Several large, gaping entrances, big enough to accommodate three men shoulder-to-shoulder, dotted the mountainside. Steep, high walls led down into widening, cavernous openings. A light fog enveloped Karen and Jesse from the cold air rushing to the surface and colliding with the humid July day. The small amount of sun that made its way into the caves glinted off the sheets of ice covering the rocks and the icicles that hung everywhere like crystal stalactites.

"This is amazing," Karen exclaimed, getting down on her knees to peer into a large crevice. "It's such a shame that someone trashed it with their garbage." She pointed at a partially concealed pile of what looked like discarded paper and cardboard boxes.

"Some people just don't care," Jesse said, as though half listening to her.

Dipping her head, she craned her neck to see more of the spectacle below her. Suddenly, the dirt gave way beneath her hand, and she pitched forward. She gasped in fear.

Warm hands closed over her shoulders, catching her and holding her back. If they'd been in a crowd of people, she'd have known from the oddly familiar touch whose hands they were before she looked up to find Jesse standing over her.

"Be careful. It's a long way down to the bottom. The caves are beautiful, but very dangerous." His brown-eyed gaze locked with hers. His low voice warmed her in places that hadn't known heat for a very long time.

Was he saying she was dangerous? For several very tense moments, their gazes held. Tingles of awareness raced over her, reminding her of the kiss they'd shared the night before and igniting a need in her for more. The desire reflected in his eyes told her Jesse was thinking similar thoughts. The caves weren't the only thing on this mountain that was dangerous.

She shook off his touch and pushed herself to her feet. Brushing the dirt off her hands, she move several steps away from Jesse and scanned the vista of the lush valley nestled between the parallel mountain ranges. "I can understand why you love these mountains so much," she said. "It's so beautiful here, so quiet, so peaceful. You almost feel like you could reach up and touch the sky." Realizing how foolish and fanciful her words may have sounded, she flushed and smiled at Jesse.

He remained silent for a few moments, studying this woman who could make his breath catch with her smile, but who cared deeply enough about another human begin to travel up here and insist on walking through the ashes of a fire scene. No doubt, part of what drove her was her love for Paul, but for some reason Jesse suspected something more motivated her.

Jesse moved to block her view of the valley. "Why are you so determined to find out how Paul died?"

The question seemed to take her by surprise. "I could ask the same of you."

For a fraction of a second, Jesse considered telling her about the guilt that ate at him daily, Instead, he said, "He was my friend." He tilted his head to better read her expression. "What about you?"

Karen turned away. What was she supposed to say? *Because he's the father of my unborn child?* Was she ready to share that with the man who was creeping into her soul with his pained, lonely eyes and host of secrets?

For the first time since she'd found out she was pregnant, with the exception of telling her sister, Karen realized she wanted to share the news about the baby with someone else, but she couldn't find the words. Deep down, she knew why. She was afraid Jesse would walk away. She was afraid she'd never see him again and, for a reason she had no desire to explore right now, that scared her more than falling into the caves had.

Instead of answering Jesse, she glanced at the position of the sinking sun, and then at her watch. "It's getting late. We have a long walk back to the car, and if we want to make it before the sun goes down, we should be going." As she hurried off down the mountainside, she could feel Jesse's puzzled gaze boring into her back.

Jesse's battered SUV bumped and bounced down the badly rutted dirt road leading from the ice caves to the main highway. Occasionally, when it bottomed out on one of the deep ruts left by eroding rains, Karen had to hang onto the overhead brace to keep her seat.

Why had he decided to take this obviously little used shortcut down the mountain rather than the paved one they'd used to come up here? Was he that anxious to get rid of her? Was he as apprehensive about being stuck up here alone with her as she was of being with him?

From time to time she glanced at Jesse's' set profile. His gaze concentrated steadily on the road ahead. His jaw muscles vibrated in response to his teeth clenching and unclenching. His death grip on the steering wheel had turned his knuckles bloodless.

Suddenly the car tipped precariously, and the wheel jerked from Jesse's grip. The sound of something hitting hard against the undercarriage split the silence. Karen gasped and tightened her hold on the brace. The SUV veered to the side, throwing Karen against Jesse. As the car came to a dead stop, she quickly righted herself.

Jesse hit the steering wheel with his fist. "Damn!" Jamming the gearshift into reverse, he slowly backed up. The screech of metal rubbing against a solid surface set Karen's teeth on edge.

"What was that?"

"I'd say it was the bottom being removed from my car," Jesse ground out. When he'd maneuvered the car to the side, he checked the road ahead of them. "Rock," was all he said, then put the car in drive and eased it out of the rut that had grabbed the tires.

"Do you think it did any damage?"

"We'll soon find out. Right now, we need to get off the mountain. It'll be dark soon and aside from being mostly deserted, these roads are even harder to travel then. If we're going to break down, I want it to be on paved highway and closer to an inhabited area so we can get help."

They both fell silent. Jesse kept his attention on the road. Karen listened with her heart in her throat for any sound that would forecast the damage done by the rock's handiwork. She took to repeating a silent prayer that the SUV would make it back to Bristol.

Sitting in close proximity to Jesse and feeling his magnetism emanating over her was bad enough. The very last thing she needed was to be stranded overnight on this mountain with Jesse Kingston. Her traitorous mind immediately began creating images of being nestled against Jesse for warmth, his hot breath brushing her face, his arms cradling her close against his muscular body, his . . . .

Jesse glanced at Karen. What was she thinking? Was she reminiscing about Paul and their life together? A life that could never be, now? Was she trying to imagine his last moments?

Though he hated himself for it, a pang of jealously mixed with guilt shot through him. What would she say when he told her he could have stopped Paul, but let his duty to his superior stand in the way? And what would she say if he told her that the life she'd planned with Paul had never had a future because he'd already had a wife and a life totally separate from the one he'd lead with Karen? Or did she already know that?

From what he'd seen of Karen in the last few days, he didn't think of her as the "other woman" type. She seemed too honorable for that, too aware of family to be the one to break up another woman's home. Maybe it was time he found out.

Just as he opened his mouth to speak the words that could destroy Karen's perception of the man she loved, he noticed the brakes had become soft. Living in the mountains and traveling roads that often descended at steep angles, he'd always made sure his brakes were in top shape. He lifted the pressure of his foot and reapplied it.

The pedal felt spongy and depressed much farther than normal. The rock must have punctured the brake line, and he was probably losing brake fluid. He immediately lifted his foot. The less pressure, the less fluid would be pumped out on the road. From the feel of the brakes, it had to be the front lines. Thankfully, the back brakes seemed to be helping to slow their forward motion. Because of the road conditions, he'd had to go slow. If he'd been on the paved road, they never would have made it to the bottom.

"As to whether or not the rock did damage . . . the answer to your question is yes." Not daring to take his eyes off the road, he spoke to the windshield instead of looking at Karen. He refrained from telling her what the problem was. No sense scaring her any more than she was already until he knew for sure what had happened.

Karen held her breath. Did this mean the car was about to break down and that they'd be trapped up here on this deserted, isolated mountain? Alone? She prayed that wouldn't be the case, that Jesse could perform a simple fix and get them back to Bristol. Deep inside, she suspected it would take a small miracle to fix whatever the problem was.

Fear gathered in her throat as she envisioned the car careening down the mountain, bouncing off the ruts and plowing into a rock or a tree. He pulled the car to the roadside and engaged the emergency brake to hold them on the hill. A lump of dread formed in her stomach.

She listened to the even throb of the engine. No lights flashed at them from the dashboard. "What is it?" she asked, her voice giving away her apprehension.

"I don't know. I have to check." He opened the car door and climbed out. Kneeling on the ground, her peered beneath the car. "Damn!"

Karen sighed. That didn't sound good. "What is it?"

Jesse, stood and then got back into the SUV. "The rock ripped open the brake line. We're losing fluid."

"I take it that's bad." As the words left her lips, she realized how stupid they'd sounded and expect some snide remark from Jesse, but, unlike what Paul would have done, none came.

He turned to her, his forehead creased in a frown. "Only if you consider *bad* to be going down this mountain with only half the braking system working."

"So, what do we do?" The knot in her stomach doubled in size.

"Well, we can't stay here. This road sees very little traffic, for obvious reasons." He looked around him. "I have a friend who has a cabin not far from here. If we can get there, maybe he can give us a ride into town. I'll have Henry Daniels tow the car in tomorrow."

"Can you do that? Get down this mountain?" Despite her efforts to put on a brave front, Karen's voice quivered. "Without brakes?"

"We still have rear brakes, somewhat. They won't stop us, but along with the emergency brake, they'll help to slow us down." He stared deep into her eyes and saw her suppressed fear. He took her hand and squeezed it reassuringly. "I'll try my best to make sure nothing happens to you."

For a long moment, their gazes held. A need foreign to Jesse rose up and overpowered him. The words he'd just spoken were not a hollow promise. He would give his life to protect this woman.

Jesse released her hand with a final reassuring squeeze, took a deep breath, and eased off the emergency brake. Using it and the increasingly ineffective spongy brake pedal to control their speed, he maneuvered the car down the steep, rutted road.

Several minutes later, he hit the brake and the pedal went to the floor. The car began to pick up speed. Using the emergency brake only, he slowed their forward momentum and guided the car through the gathering twilight. Just ahead, he could see a light and then the cabin of his friend, Dave Andrews, came into view. Jesse guided the car into the driveway, then yanked on the emergency brake.

Despite her attempt to hide it behind her hand, he heard Karen's sigh of relief. Feeling his own tension ease, he couldn't blame her. He wasn't sure his relief stemmed totally from making it off the mountain alive or from being saved from spending the entire night with a woman who, if allowed, could tempt him far beyond his limits of control? But, if he wanted to be honest with himself, would spending a night with Karen have been that bad? If he went exclusively by his body's reaction to just considering it, he'd have to admit that the appeal of such an eventuality was much more powerful than he'd expected.

"Jesse, my boy!"

Dave Andrew's voice roused Jesse from his contemplation. The short, somewhat overweight man hurried toward them. Jesse swung the SUV's door open, stepped from the car and grasped the older man's outstretched hand. "Hey, Dave."

"Didn't hear you drive up. I was just on my way to the mailbox to put this in it." He indicated a white envelope clutched in his hand. "That can wait." Dave eyed the woman getting out of the passenger side of the SUV. "Who's your friend?"

"Karen Ellis, this is Dave Andrews. God put Dave on this mountain right after he fashioned it out of rock and dirt." They laughed.

Dave had been here long before Jesse arrived, but he was a fast friend to all the rangers and most of them made a habit of stopping off here for a cup of Dave's stronger-than-turpentine coffee when they were in the neighborhood. He'd took them hunting and fishing with him and taught several of the guys how to tie trout flies.

The old man grasped Karen's hand. "My pleasure, little lady." Then over his shoulder to Jesse, he said, "I have to say that your choice of companions has vastly improved, Kingston." He turned back to Karen. "Most times he comes around here dragging along some dirt-ugly ranger."

Jesse noted the flush that turned Karen's cheeks a becoming shade of pink. He opened his mouth to explain why they were there, but Karen took Dave's offered hand and laughed nervously.

"You'll have to excuse me while I catch my breath. Coming down off that mountain without brakes kind of left me speechless," Karen explained, making light of what Jesse was sure had been a harrowing experience for her.

Dave arched one of his white, bushy eyebrows. "Oh?" He stepped aside. "Well, come on inside, and we'll call Henry Daniels to come get the car. Probably won't be until morning though." Dave chuckled. "He's the only game in town, so to speak, and he has no qualms about closing up at five and not opening again for anybody." Not waiting for Jesse, Dave enclosed Karen's elbow in his palm and guided her up the steps to the cabin. "Folks around here know better than to break down when it's past Henry's business hours."

Once inside, they settled into the well-worn but comfortable sofa in front of the blackened fireplace. Jesse called Henry while Dave started supper. Dave was right. Henry said he'd pick up the SUV first thing the next day and, no matter how much Jesse begged, not before, leaving them stranded.

"No problem. I'll take the two of you back. We'll drop Karen at Mildred's B&B and then take you home. But first, this young lady looks like she could use a good meal, so we're gonna have something to eat." Jesse opened his mouth to decline the invitation, but Dave raised a hand to silence him. "That isn't up for a vote."

"I didn't realize how hungry I was." Karen sighed contentedly and leaned back in her chair. "I'm so glad you persuaded us to stay for dinner."

Dave stood and removed the empty plates from the table. "My pleasure." He carried the stacked dishes toward the small kitchen. "Coffee?"

Jesse jumped to his feet, intercepted him and took the dirty dishes. "You cooked dinner. I can serve coffee."

Without argument, Dave returned to the table and in moments had plunged deep into conversation with Karen. Jesse couldn't hear what they were saying, but he could hear Karen's laughter from time to time. It seemed to fill the room. Each burst rippled over him like mountain spring water, washing away the tension that had held his body prisoner for so long.

He leaned his hip against the counter and watched her. She was talking animatedly with Dave as though she'd known him all her life. How he envied her ability to relate to people. How he wished he could be that open, that real, that unguarded.

Karen laughed again and a wave of peace flowed over him. Her gaze moved from Dave to Jesse. She smiled. A part of him that had been content to live in the isolation of loneliness came to life and struggled toward the warmth of her light. This woman was becoming more important, more a part of him with every passing moment. And he wasn't at all sure he wanted to fight it anymore.

Dave pulled his pickup truck to a stop in front of the Land of Nod Bed and Breakfast. Karen was sad to see the ride end. After the day they'd had, the strength of Jesse's thigh pressed against hers for the last hour had been comforting, reassuring.

She turned to look at him. He made no move to open the door and let her out. Instead, his gaze held hers. She could almost feel his invitation to share another kiss and wished that Dave would evaporate so they could act on it.

"You kids want me to take a walk around the block?"

Dave's voice broke the spell holding her trapped in Jesse's

eyes. Jesse blinked and then fumbled with the truck's door handle before he finally opened it and then climb down to let her out.

"Mind your own business, old man." Jesse softened the reprimand with a smile.

Dave chuckled. "Just trying to help."

Karen planted a quick kiss on Dave's cheek. "Thanks for everything. I hope I see you again before I leave."

"Good Lord willing," Dave said.

Karen jumped down, threw a longing look at Jesse, then hurried up the path to the quaint Victorian style house.

Dave made no move to start the truck. Instead, he stared after Karen. When she'd disappeared inside the house, he turned to Jesse. "You up for some advice?"

The question surprised Jesse. At a loss as to what to say, he tried to make light of it. "Not unless you plan on sending me to that the fishing hole at Walter's Creek again, which was supposedly crawling with trout."

Dave smiled, but Jesse had the feeling it wasn't heartfelt. "Well you'd have known I was lying if you just used the brain God gave you. Fish don't crawl."

Jesse laughed, but he stopped when Dave's expression turned serious. "What's up, Dave?"

A heavy sigh escaped from Jesse's friend. "I don't make it a habit to stick my nose in where it has no business being, but I like you, boy, and I'm gonna make an exception. I got two pieces of advice for you." He pointed toward the house into which Karen had just disappeared. "That little lady is special, very special. I ain't denying that you had a rough upbringing, but Frank Kingston turned to dust long ago and those two sisters of yours think you're the greatest thing since fire. Don't let that young lady get away because of that wall you've built around your heart."

Jesse made no immediate reply. He looked down at his hands and recalled the wash of peace that had overcome him when he'd listened to Karen's laughter. But even now, he had no desire to discuss with Dave or anyone else these new feelings coursing through him. Too much still lay between him and Karen to even consider allowing his emotions to take control of his head.

"And what's the second piece of advice."

Dave started the truck's engine and for a moment Jesse didn't think the old man was going to answer him, but he didn't put the truck in gear. Instead he stared out the windshield as if deciding if he wanted to say more.

Then Dave cleared his throat. "I know you been talking to the other guys about how Paul died, and you need to stop. There's folks on that mountain who won't take kindly to it."

Chapter 6

The next morning, while on his way to stop by the garage to check on his car then pick up Karen before driving to the Albany airport to meet her sister, Jesse was still thinking about Dave's veiled warning. He hadn't been able to talk the old man into expanding on what he'd said. In fact, Dave had closed up tighter than a clam. He'd dropped Jesse off at Emily's house so he could borrow her car, then with nothing more than a "See ya," drove away.

That didn't mean Jesse could or would easily forget the ominous ring to what the older man had said. In fact, in Jesse's mind, Dave's warning all but confirmed for him that Paul's death was more than an accident caused by a seasoned ranger's bad judgment as Hank had said.

If nothing questionable had happened then why would anyone be upset with him digging for answers? And exactly who were the "folks on the mountain" who would not "take kindly" to Jesse and Karen nosing around the burn site?

Jesse still hadn't found the answer when he pulled Emily's car up next to Henry's Garage. Inside the repair shop, he found his SUV perched high in the air on the lift. The smell of oil, gasoline, and grease greeted him. Henry was under the car, looking thoughtfully at the area behind the front wheel.

"Hey, Henry," Jesse called.

At the greeting, Henry ducked his head and peered around the tire. His grease-streaked face broke into a wide grin. "Hey."

"I take it the car's not fixed yet."

Henry glanced back at the SUV. "Oh, it's fixed. I was just checkin' to make sure there was no other damage."

"And?"

He shoved his grimy baseball cap back, itched his head, then readjusted it. "Well, far's I can see, it's okay." Jesse cringed at the unspoken *but* hanging on the end of that sentence. Henry shoved his hand in the pocket of his greasy coveralls, withdrew a rag as grimy as his hands, and wiped them on it, then tucked it behind the overalls' bib. "There's somethin' you need to see."

Jesse waited while Henry went to his workbench to retrieve something. He returned to where Jesse waited and handed it to him. In Jesse's palm lay a length of what looked like the rubber tubing that connected the stainless steel brake line to the wheel hub. In the side of the tube was a neat slice about one-quarter inch long.

"I ain't no forensic scientist, Jesse, but I've seen my share of ruptured brake lines and brake lines torn apart by rough roads, and I'd stake my reputation on it that that tube didn't just bust and that no rock did that." Harry shook his head. "No sireee. Somebody cut that." He frowned. "Somebody didn't want you and that pretty friend of yours comin' down off the mountain in one piece."

All the way to the B&B Jesse thought about what Henry had said. Though he wanted to believe otherwise, he couldn't help but feel Henry was right. Not a doubt lingered that the tubing had been cut on purpose. Dave's warning took on an even more ominous tone.

As Jesse pulled up in front of The Land of Nod Bed and Breakfast, he was still searching his mind for who could have done such a thing. Right away, he noticed Karen ready and waiting, legs crossed, sitting in one of the half dozen white rocking chairs that dotted the front porch. His mind went blank to everything except her exceptional beauty. Like a schoolboy, he gawked as she waved, then rose gracefully from the chair and walked down the path toward him.

The morning sun shone off her hair turning it to white gold. His imagination kicked in with a vengeance.

Without warning, he was transported from the car to the king-sized bed in his bedroom. He was running his fingers through Karen's hair while her naked body clung to his in the throes of passionate lovemaking. Her long legs coiled around his thighs, and her hot breath fanned his cheeks. Jesse couldn't distinguish if it was his moans of desire that filled his ears or hers. Tingles of pleasure flooded him as her hands—

The *click* of the car's door latch opening snatched him from his erotic daydream.

"Good morning." Karen slid into the passenger seat. Her soft perfume instantly filled the car's interior. "Isn't it a beautiful day?"

Jesse blinked. He opened the window on his side and breathed deeply of the fresh, unscented air that rushed in. Shifting his suddenly painful position in the seat, he cleared his throat, and then started the car. He had to stop this. He had more important things to think about than jumping Karen's bones.

His friend was dead, and it was looking more and more like it wasn't the accident everyone thought it was. Everyone except him and Karen.

"If you say so," he mumbled. "I hadn't noticed." When she didn't offer any response, he stole a sidelong glance at her. Should he tell her what he knew?

She was staring questioningly at him.

He paused in the act of shifting the car into gear. "What?"

She shrugged. "You're a complicated man, Jesse Kingston."

This time he turned and looked directly at her. "What makes you say that?"

She smiled. "You like to make people think you're distant and unconcerned with life around you, but you aren't. Not really. You see much more than you'd like the rest of us to believe you do, and you do it from a safe emotional distance."

Stunned that she was able to read him so accurately when no one else had even made the effort to understand him, he covered his surprise with a sarcastic chuckle and shifted the car into gear. "The lady is a psychic."

She laughed that laugh that slipped under his skin and shot hot arrows throughout his blood. "No, not psychic. Just insightful. You hide your feelings well, but in the end, I'll figure you out."

Since he'd never been able to figure himself out, he doubted that, but it would keep her busy. However, deep down, he had a strange feeling that Karen did see things in him he'd never exposed to anyone else and that scared the bejesus out of him. The last thing he needed right now was for this woman, who held an undeniable attraction for him, to slip any farther under his skin.

"I stopped by to see if my car was fixed." He paused, still unsure if he should say anything. Then again, how could he not say anything? Her life had been in danger last night as well as his, and she was just as suspicious of Paul's death as he was. She deserved to know.

"And was it?" She tilted her head to look at him and a cascade of white blonde hair fell over her shoulder. Before his erotic fantasies could kick in again, he told her what he'd found out and there was no way to sugarcoat it.

"Karen, when we bottomed out yesterday on the way off the mountain, we didn't damage the brake lines. Someone cut them." He told her about Dave's warning and what Henry had found. He glanced at Karen for her reaction.

"My God! Are you sure? " A cold, foreboding chill shivered over her.

Jesse nodded. "I know a cut when I see it, and Henry confirmed it." He took a deep breath. "Add that to what Dave told me, and the only conclusion we can draw is that someone didn't want us to get off the mountain alive."

"When could anyone have done such a thing? And why would they do it?"

"I figure it was done while we were at the ice caves, and the car was unattended and not many people come up there so there was little chance of being caught. Someone could have easily slashed them then and never been seen." He sighed. "The only conclusion I can see is that someone is afraid we're going to find out something they don't want us to know. Like how Paul really died."

Though the thoughts of anyone trying to harm her and Jesse chilled her to the bone, it also made Karen more determined than ever to find out exactly why Paul Jackson died in the wildfire.

"So, aside from Dave's warning and the cut brake lines, we really don't have any concrete evidence that there was anything shady about Paul's death." Karen summed up what they knew for Elle in the car on their way from the Albany airport. "Just gut feelings. We don't even know if they're connected."

"Well, what you've told me sounds pretty damned incriminating for someone, and that someone is determined you don't find out what they're hiding," Elle said. "Let's go take a look at the fire site."

"Don't you want to stop at the motel first?" Jesse asked.

Elle shook her head. "The site has been open to the elements long enough. I'd like see it as soon as possible, and there's no time like the present."

"You got it." Jesse took the next exit ramp off the Thruway and headed north.

Karen glanced over her shoulder at her sister. "Do you think there may still be something in the ashes that will be more conclusive, some clue that was left behind that will give us a direction?"

"If anyone can find it, Elle can," Elle's husband, Scott Banks, put in. He smiled down at his wife, then slid his arm around her shoulders and pulled her close. "She's got a nose like a bloodhound for this stuff."

Elle frowned and elbowed her husband gently in the ribs. "Is that your idea of a compliment, Banks?"

Everyone, including, to Karen's surprise, Jesse, laughed.

Karen had been stunned when Scott got off the plane with Elle. Her sister had quickly explained that she thought her detective husband might be of use with some of the non-fire details. Karen suspected it was more because he didn't want to be away from his fairly-new wife for so long. Using the love that glowed in his eyes when he looked at Elle as a point of reference, Karen thought it spoke volumes for their relationship.

One day, God willing, Karen would find that kind of devotion in a man. She was slowly realizing that whatever else she'd had with Paul, it hadn't been that. She'd always wondered if Paul had been as committed to their relationship as she had. But she'd consigned her misgivings to the remnants of her childhood paranoia about her being low man on the totem pole when it came to her importance in other people's lives. Just for once, she'd wanted to be at the top of the list. By ignoring Paul's hot and cold running attitude toward their future together, she'd been able to be just that . . . at least in her own mind.

Her gaze shifted to Jesse's profile. Was this the man who would one day look at her with the love in his eyes that Scott displayed when he looked at Elle? Was Jesse the man who could give her that kind of devotion?

As with so many of the questions she had about Jesse, these also remained unanswered. Jesse had some of the same attributes that she'd found so hard to live with in Paul: an unwavering love of the his job above all else, a reluctance to share himself with others, and the ability to close off his deepest emotions. Did she really want to have to deal with all that again?

Oddly, the aversion she'd expected to feel at the idea of a relationship with Jesse never materialized. Somewhere deep inside, she knew that the man he presented to those around him was not the man he kept hidden underneath that cold exterior. She had no idea why she felt that way, just that she did. But what if her gut feelings were wrong?

Besides, there was also one other thing she had to consider. Her hand slid over her stomach. This baby needed a family, an identity, loving parents. Could Jesse give it that? Could—

She brought her thoughts to a halt. Whatever made her even believe that she and Jesse had a future, that he even cared about her in that way, or that what she'd been feeling for him was anything more than gratitude? That question raised another more pressing one—why was it she was so uncertain about Jesse's feelings and not her own?

Before she could explore that, Jesse pulled the car into the parking lot next to the footpath that would take them to the burn site.

Dark clouds hung over the mountains, and Karen wondered if Elle would have a chance to complete her investigation before the sky opened up and they had to leave it for another day. Undaunted by the impending storm, Elle picked up her case and trudged forward, seemingly unaware of nature's threat or the fire stench that still clung tenaciously to the landscape.

Never having seen Elle at work before, Karen watched in awe as her beauty-queen sister transformed before her eyes into a trained arson investigator. When they were kids, if anyone had told her that one day she'd stand in a burned-out section of woods and watch her gorgeous sister digging in the blackened, charred dirt, Karen would have thought them crazy. But, amazingly, that's exactly what Elle was doing.

As Elle attacked a particularly black pile of charred debris, Karen couldn't hold back the grin. Their mother must be spinning in her grave.

Elle lifted a spade full of the damp earth to her face and smelled it. "This site is pretty old and has been washed thoroughly by rain, but I think I can detect traces of gasoline," she announced and deposited what was on the shovel in a metal canister and then sealed and labeled it. "Jesse, did they set backfire here?"

Jesse shook his head. "Not to my knowledge. Are you sure it's gas?"

Elle shrugged. "Until the lab takes a stab at it, it's just my guess. We'll know for sure after it's analyzed." She went back to checking out the burn site.

Karen and Jesse exchanged satisfied glances. If Elle was right, then maybe they had good basis for their suspicions. Karen opened her mouth to say so, but Scott touched her arm and shook his head.

"She won't hear you. When she does this, it's as if she's in another world. It claims every bit of her attention and concentration." He grinned, then readjusted Elle's camera strap on his shoulder. "Actually, it's quite the awesome process to watch." Pride colored his expression and his tone.

Scott was right. While he, Karen, and Jesse stood silently to the side, Elle continued her methodical investigation of the scene as if they weren't there. She turned over leaves, scraped the bark off trees, dug into the dark soil, and cut samples from the charred vegetation.

Seemingly happy with what she'd collected, Elle moved beyond the burned-out area. The underbrush outside the perimeter of the fire-damaged trees had continued to grow and was a couple of feet high. Karen smiled when that didn't deter Elle. Like parting her hair, she pushed it flat to inspect what lay beneath it.

Suddenly, Elle put aside her sample case and got to her knees. Karen stiffened. Had Elle found something? She watched as her sister crawled along the ground in a straight line for about four or five feet, pushing the underbrush out of her way. They waited, then moved to where Elle knelt.

Jesse squatted down next to Elle and then ran his fingers over the indentation Elle had discovered in the ground. "What is it?"

At first, Elle didn't answer him, then blinking, as if arousing from a dream, she sighed. "No idea. Maybe nothing, but I'll take a photograph and send it to be analyzed along with the other debris I've collected. Hold the grass back, Jesse." She straightened and took her camera from Scott then snapped several photos from several angles. When she'd finished, she handed the camera back to her husband and then picked up her sample case. "That's about all I can do for now, except talk to anyone with knowledge of the fire itself." As Scott quietly slipped the case from her hand, she turned to Jesse. "If I go by the ranger station, will your boss be in? I'd like to ask him a few questions about the fire"

"He should be. Do you want me to call him?"

Elle shook her head. "No. Drop us at the motel. You can give us his phone number and directions to the ranger station, and we'll borrow Karen's car and drive there. I'll call from my cell on the way." She turned to Karen. "I'm assuming I can borrow your car."

Karen nodded. "Jesse's brother-in-law did a minor repair on it and said he'd drop it by later tonight. I'll call him and have him bring it straight to the motel." She pulled out her cell and dialed Emily's number as Jesse recited it.

While she was busy talking to Emily, Jesse recited Hank's number from memory as Elle jotted it down on a small pad she'd pulled from her evidence case.

As they all walked back to the car, unable to remain quiet any longer, Karen asked, "So what do you think?"

Elle stopped walking and turned to her sister. She released her hair from the clip that had confined it during the investigation and shook it loose. "As a rule, I don't voice any preliminary conclusions, but because you're my sister, I'll tell you this. I've been in this business for a while and when there's no parking lot, no residence, no backfire, and no other reason for it, finding traces of gasoline near a fire scene raises some serious questions in my mind."

"You think it's arson?" Jesse had come up behind them.

Elle glanced at him and then at Karen. "Just between us? If I had to stake my job on it, I'd say yes." She continued walking and stumbled over an exposed root. Scott was quick to grab her elbow and steady her. "Thanks, Banks, but I'm pregnant, not breakable."

He kissed her cheek. "I know." Giving her a loving pat on her behind, he hurried toward the car.

"Pregnant?" Karen all but screamed.

Elle threw Scott a reprimanding glance, then nodded and grinned. "Yes. About two and a half months. Sorry you had to find out that way. I was going to tell you, but we haven't had a moment alone to really get into any sister-to-sister talk."

"I'm so thrilled for you, Elle." She hugged her sister. "Our babies will be able to be playmates."

Karen realized what she'd just said and quickly looked around to see if Jesse had overheard it. She sighed when she saw that Jesse had gone ahead to congratulate Scott and help him stow Elle's gear in the trunk.

Elle stepped in front of Karen, blocking her path. Elle's smile faded. "What about you? Have you told Jesse?"

Karen shook her head. "I will . . . when the time is right." She glanced anywhere but at Elle's stern expression. "It's not like he's the father."

"He's not?"

Karen shook her head again. "It's Paul's."

Elle stepped in front of her. "I saw the way Jesse looks at you, and he deserves to know, Karen."

No answer she wanted to confide in her sister came to mind. Stepping past Elle, Karen continued toward the car. She'd known for a long time why she hadn't told Jesse. Not all men wanted ready-made families. Jesse could very well be one of them, and she didn't want him to walk out of her life. But she also knew, the longer she stayed around, the more evident her condition would become and then she'd be left no choice.

Chapter 7

Jesse maneuvered the car down Bristol's Main Street toward the B&B. It was well past ten o'clock, and, as Emily's mother-in-law always used to say when Jesse was a kid, the streets had been rolled up for the night. They paused at the blinking red light in the middle of town. Their car was the only one in sight. The total lack of noise in the street reflected that of the interior of their car.

Ever since they'd dropped Elle and Scott at the motel a few miles north of town, the atmosphere in the car had changed. A pregnant silence had replaced the previous lively conversation that the four of them had been engaged in. Though neither Jesse nor Karen had said a word, Jesse knew that, like him, Karen had to be mentally analyzing what Elle had said.

If there could be no other reasonable explanation for gasoline being present in those woods, then it had to have been brought there and chances were pretty good that it was used as an accelerant to add fuel to the deadly wildfire. But why?

Jesse already knew that the fire had been started by a careless camper west of where Paul had died. With the brisk crosswind they'd been fighting that day, why would anyone want to make an out-of-control blaze even deadlier? And what did Paul have to do with any of it? Was it as simple as him being in the wrong place at the wrong time? Jesse didn't think so.

Karen's sigh drew him from his thoughts. From his peripheral vision, he could see her fold her hands over her stomach, close her eyes and lay her head against the headrest. Before their trip to the burn site, Jesse had planned to tell Karen about Paul's marriage on the way home. Now, however, he could see that the day had taken a heavy toll on her. He put off the conversation until another time.

A few moments later Jesse pulled the car to stop beside the curb in front of The Land of Nod B&B. "I'll walk you up."

"That's not necessary." Half-sleep thickened Karen's voice and turned it to an enticing, husky temptation.

"That wasn't a question." He pulled the keys from the ignition and opened his door.

Karen grabbed his arm. "Jesse, I—" She didn't want him to feel responsible for her. But, contrarily, she loved that he did.

Sighing, he turned to her and covered her hand with his. "Someone tried to make sure we didn't get off that mountain yesterday, Karen. I am not about to let you walk into a dark house by yourself. End of discussion." He smiled. "I told you I'd do my best to protect you, and that still goes."

Warmth rushed everywhere in her body. No one had ever wanted to protect her. Just the thought turned her all soft inside. It reminded her of how Scott had watched over Elle when she tripped over the root. Suddenly, Jesse protecting her seemed very right.

"Okay." She slipped from the car and started up the front walk with Jesse at her side, her elbow cupped in his warm palm.

Karen inserted her key in her room's lock. The tumblers clicked into place, but before she opened the door, she leaned forward and kissed Jesse's cheek lightly. "Thank you."

He said nothing, just touched the spot she'd kissed, stared intently into her eyes and then shook his head and turned on his heel to leave. Sending one last glance in his direction, she opened the door . . . and screamed.

Jesse was at her side instantly. "Wha—" The question was never voiced completely.

Karen could say nothing. All she could do was look around her trashed room. Clothes lay everywhere on the floor, the bed and the furniture. Her cosmetics were strewn over the bed. The vanity chair lay on its side, half concealed beneath the bedspread, which had been torn from the bed and thrown to the floor.

Emotions cascaded through her like water over a steep

precipice. Her skin crawled. She rubbed her bare arms with shaking hands, trying to fight down the feeling of being trashed physically as much as the room had been literally.

Fear, stark and blood-freezing, anchored her to the spot. "Who could have done this?" Her whispered voice shook with the onslaught of terror that had claimed her entire body.

Jesse rushed past her and began gathering her clothes. He snatched her suitcases from the closet and threw clothes into them. "We'll worry about that later. Right now, you're coming home with me."

Until then Karen had only been able to stare in openmouthed awe at the sight before her. But his words mobilized her. "I'm what?" She'd heard what he said, but a sane reply escaped her.

"You can't stay here. You're coming home with me. No arguments. When we get to my house, we'll call the police and report it." His voice shook almost as much as hers and his complexion had turned pale.

He gathered her cosmetics, threw them in the middle of the snarl of clothing, checked the room for anything he may have missed, and then snapped the suitcases closed. Snatching them off the bed, he turned to her. "Let's go."

For a moment, she balked. An inane tangle of words, thoughts, and questions raced through her mind. None of them made sense to her, but she couldn't seem to stem the flow.

Should he have touched anything before the police came? Did she want to stay with him? Where would she go instead? Had he gotten all her cosmetics off the bed? Who would tell her landlady she was leaving? And Elle? Who would tell Elle?

"Karen." Jesse put down the suitcases and grabbed her arms. "Karen, listen to me." He shook her gently, rousing her from her stupor. "You have no other choice."

"I can go stay at the motel with Elle and Scott."

He grabbed her by the shoulders. She could feel his hands shaking. "I can't protect you if you're in the motel." He sighed. "I'd feel better if you're with me."

She could hear the fear thickening his voice. Dumbly, Karen nodded. "Okay," she final managed.

As they raced toward his house, Jesse threw repeated glances at Karen. Huddled in the corner of the seat, she looked like a frightened child. With the aid of the dashboard lights, he could see her tightly clenched hands trembling in her lap and her pale complexion. Despite the warmth of the July night, by the time he pulled into his driveway, her shivering had become worse. Shock.

Once inside, he found a blanket and used it to wrap her in a warm cocoon, then guided her to the sofa. He tucked the blanket securely around her. "I'm going to call the police and then make coffee. Will you be okay?"

To his surprise, she smiled and nodded. As he turned to walk away, she clutched at his hand. "You'll take care of us?"

"Always." He squeezed her hand reassuringly and then went to make the phone call to the authorities.

Not until after the police had arrived and taken his and Karen's statement and then left, did Jesse have time to register what Karen had said. *Us.* She asked if he'd take care of *us*. What an odd thing to say. Had she meant *them*? Him and Karen?

He closed the front door behind the police, then went to sit beside Karen on the couch. "How ya doing?" She'd stopped shaking, and her complexion had regained some of the color it had lost when she'd stepped into that room and saw the mess.

"Better," she said and gave him a forced smile. "What do you think they were looking for?"

Jesse shook his head. "Beats me. Maybe they thought we'd found something, and you had it in your room."

"Why didn't anyone hear them trashing the room and stop them, and how did they get in?" Her voice held a fanatic edge.

He closed his hand over hers. He'd sell his soul to have been able to spare her that intimate intrusion into her life. But since it was a done deal, he had to settle for just being here for her now and protecting her from a repeat. "For now, let's let the police worry about that. I'm sure they'll fill us in when they know anything."

She grew silent, and Jesse knew she was still dwelling on the questions she'd asked. His mind, however, went back to what she'd said before he called the police.

He swung around to face her squarely. "What did you mean before when you ask me if I'd take care of *us*? Who's *us*?"

Karen stiffened and averted her gaze to study her hands, which were once more clenched in her lap. The word *us* had slipped out, and when he hadn't reacted to it, she'd hoped he hadn't heard it. She'd been wrong. Very wrong. The moment she'd dreaded since she first met Jesse was staring her straight in the face. Now that it was here, how did she tell him? It was almost like trying to tell someone that their dearest friend had died and do it without causing them emotional upset. There didn't seem to be any easy way to say it or to prepare him for it.

Plucking up her courage, she summoned the right words. A sinking desperation filled her. Finally, she just blurted it out before she lost her nerve. "I'm three and a half months pregnant with Paul's child."

Jesse stared at her. Apprehension coiled in a tight knot inside her. Why didn't he say something? Anything. She couldn't read his expression. Was it disbelief? Anger?

When she could stand his silence no longer, she reached for his arm. He pulled back from her touch. The pain that shot through her had to be her heart cracking open. "Jesse?"

Slamming his fist on the table, he jumped to his feet. "Dammit!"

The crack in her heart widened and bled. It was just as she'd feared all along. He didn't want to be involved with a woman who was carrying another man's baby. In this case, it just happened to be his best friend's baby.

Explain. Tell him why you wanted to keep it a secret. He'll understand. He has to understand.

"Jesse, I—" Karen reached for him again, but he'd already moved beyond her fingertips. Hopefully, her secretiveness hadn't pushed him beyond compassion, too.

Jesse glanced at her, shook his head, as though nothing she could say would make it right again, then, without another word, he strode from the room.

Chapter 8

Jesse lay on his bed trying to wrap his mind around Karen's shocking announcement. Pregnant with Paul's child. That was something he didn't need to hear. Now, how was he supposed to tell her that Paul was married? How was he supposed to tell her that the father of her unborn child was a cheat and a liar? That he'd dishonored a woman who had come to quickly mean a great deal to Jesse. He'd always known Paul had a tendency to be self-absorbed, but Jesse never dreamed he'd go this far.

"Damn you, Paul!"

Jesse got up and paced the room. He'd been taught not to speak ill of the dead, but he was finding it very difficult to find forgiveness for what Paul had done. Increasingly over the last few days, Jesse had become more and more convinced that Karen had no idea about Paul's marital status and that she was an innocent victim of a man who had no respect for his marriage vows.

Now, Paul had gotten himself killed, and Jesse had been thrust into a position to mop up the mess he'd left behind. Anger filled him. Anger at a man who thought he could burn the candle at both ends and not care if he hurt anyone. Anger at a man who thought only of himself and gave not a thought to the pain he was inflicting on the women in his life. Anger at being forced into the position of having to be the one to tell Karen.

Taking a deep breath, Jesse bolstered himself to tell Karen about Paul, but as he started to leave the bedroom, the bedside phone rang.

"Hello."

"Jesse, it's Butch Haskell."

Butch was one of the rangers Jesse worked with, but they'd

never been the kind of friends that he and Paul had been. Butch had been injured recently in a fire and had been assigned to office duty. This out-of-the-blue phone call didn't make sense to Jesse. Why was Butch calling him?

"Hey, Butch, what's up?" Jesse sat on the edge of the bed.

"I wanted to give you a heads-up. Hank just met with that lady arson investigator from Florida. I overheard everything. He's mad as a hornet that you brought her in to look at the fire scene. He's raving about sending you home to get your head on straight, and it was never gonna happen if you didn't let this thing go." Pause. "Jesse, he's talking about firing you."

Jesse's back stiffened. "Firing me?"

"Yup. Says he doesn't want anyone around here who can't follow orders. Says this is state land, and a Florida arson investigator has no jurisdiction here. He ordered her to stay off the land."

Jesse vaulted to his feet. "He can order all he wants. That's state land, but he's forgetting that it's also public land. Unless there's a danger to the public and it's posted off limits, he can't keep anyone out."

Butch sighed. "I know that and you know that, but, Jesse, he's not happy, and he's gonna try to stop her from going back there. He's asked me to file a request with the higher ups to have it declared off limits to the public due to safety issues from the fire."

Jesse ran his fingers through his hair. Frustration fueled his anger. "When are you filing the paperwork, and how long will it take to go through the system?"

Jesse could hear Butch shuffling papers. "I'm supposed to file it tomorrow. Should take a day or two."

"Can you stall it?" They had to have time for Elle to complete her investigation.

A heavy sigh came through the phone. "Geeze, Jesse. In the mood he's in, I'd be taking a big chance."

"Butch, this is important. Please? I'll owe you." Jesse suddenly remembered something that might convince Butch. "I'll personally introduce you to that cute little clerk at the trading post. The one you been dying to meet."

Long pause. "That's playing dirty, Jesse."

Jesse laughed. His impatience made it sound brittle. "Yeah. What do you say? Deal?"

Long pause. "Okay. I guess it can get lost on my desk for a few days. Two at the most. I can't promise any more than that."

"Thanks. And Butch? Why did you decide to let me know what was happening?"

Another pause hung heavy on the air before Butch spoke into the phone again. "Because I heard what that arson investigator was telling Hank, and she convinced me that there's something fishy going on. And while I'm spilling my guts and putting my own job on the chopping block . . . there's something else you should know."

Jesse waited, unsure of what else Butch could have to say, but relieved that someone other than he and Karen found the circumstances of Paul's death suspicious.

"That track she found in the mud? I heard her tell Hank the dimensions. There's only one thing I've ever seen leave an indentation like that. A helicopter. And you know that we didn't have any choppers out there that day, Jesse. Have her check for another landing skid print parallel to the one she found."

A door slammed in the background. "Haskell, bring today's fire reports to my office," Hank's familiar voice ordered.

"Gotta go," Butch whispered into the phone. The line went dead.

Jesse stood there holding the humming receiver for a while trying to digest what Butch had told him. This was the second person who'd warned him off. Well, they could warn him off until hell froze over. He wasn't giving up that easy, especially with all the evidence piling up that reinforced his belief that Paul's death was not an accident.

Jesse dialed Elle's motel room and related what Butch had told him. She promised to go back to the fire scene the following

72

morning and look for the other indentation as well as take measurements. In the meantime, she'd call a friend in Florida who flew the Air-Medi helicopter for the local hospital and get the specs for a chopper small enough to land in the area where she'd found the dent.

When Jesse finally emerged from the bedroom, Karen sat balled in a tight fetal position in the corner of the couch. The lamp light reflected off the moisture on her cheeks.

"Karen?"

She raised her face to him. Her eyes were red and swollen so it hadn't been just a spurt of weeping. No doubt she'd been crying the whole time he'd been gone. He could kick himself for walking out on her without explanation.

Jesse sat next to her and drew her into his arms. She came without resistance. "I'm sorry I walked out. I should have stayed and talked to you about . . . " He laid his palm on her stomach. " . . . this."

She leaned back and looked first at his hand, then at him, her expressive eyes telling him how much he'd hurt her. "Are you still angry that I didn't tell you sooner?"

He shook his head. "I was never angry that you hadn't told me."

"What then? That certainly wasn't the reaction of a man who was pleased with my news."

Jesse hesitated. He'd never have a better opportunity than now to tell her about Paul, but not wanting to add to the pain in her eyes, he continued to hold back. As upset as she was, he wasn't going to add to it. It could wait for a better time.

"A bit shocked."

"A bit? A bit doesn't send a person stomping from the room."

He grinned down at her and cupped her chin in his hand. "Okay, more than a bit."

Suddenly, talking about his abrupt exit from the room was the last thing on Jesse's mind. He stared deep into the green pools of her eyes. Unable to withstand the temptation, he ran his thumb over her bottom lip. She sucked in her breath.

He knew what he wanted to do, but his conscience stepped between him and his physical need. He couldn't put it off, he had to tell her about Paul before this went any farther. "We need to talk about—"

Shaking her head, Karen placed her fingers over his mouth. "I don't want to talk anymore." Desire saturated her husky voice.

Jesse took a deep breath and fought for control of his aroused body. "Karen, this is not a good idea. You're understandably upset and scared, probably in shock. You're doing this out of a need for reassur—"

Again she cut off his words. "I wasn't upset and scared yesterday or the day before."

What was she saying? That she had wanted then what he saw written clearly in her expression now? They'd only known each other for a few days. Could this really be happening so quickly? Then he remembered the instant, strong attraction he'd felt when they first met, the kiss they'd shared and her reaction to it. The heated looks, full of an unspoken yearning to share another kiss, that they'd exchanged over the past few days.

His blood pounded in his temples, shutting out all rational thought. Only two things broke through the haze of desire—the intense longing in Karen's eyes and the sexual tension coloring her voice.

Very slowly, he lowered his mouth to hers. The first touch shot through him like an electrical jolt. Pulling a fraction free of the contact, he hesitated. Her sweet breath fanned his skin and his mouth, and it drew him back like a magnet. At first, he feathered her lips with teasing butterfly kisses. Then she slipped her hand around to the back of his head, pulled him to her, and captured his lips with hers.

The force of her response sent his senses spiraling to heights he'd never experienced with another woman. In his lifetime, he couldn't recall anyone actually *needing* him with such incredible intensity. It rocked him to his very foundation and gave birth to hesitation.

The kind of need emanating from Karen meant emotional commitment from him and that gave rise to stark fear. Commitment was a human attribute that had always been a stumbling block to happiness for Jesse. Not because he felt incapable of it, but because, in the past, it had bought him nothing but pain.

Putting an arm's length distance between them, he pulled back and fought for an even breath. "This is not a good idea, Karen," he whispered between the breaths tearing from his aching chest.

She stared up at him with large, hurt eyes. "I—"

"It's too soon," he said, using the first excuse that came to mind. He stood, ran his fingers through his hair and tried not to look at her. "There's a spare room down the hall on the left. I've already put your suitcase in there." He glanced at her and cringed at the expression on her lovely face.

Karen continued to stare at him, her face reflecting the pain and the questions that had to be running through her mind, then without a word, she stood and went down the hall.

Jesse glanced at the illuminated face of his digital alarm clock. Three-twenty four. At this rate, he wasn't even sure why he'd bothered to come to bed. It certainly wasn't because he was getting any sleep. Between the newest developments in the clues about what had really happened to Paul and the encounter he'd had with Karen on the couch, his mind and his body weren't interested in anything even resembling sleep.

While the questions surrounding Paul's death were no less important to him, the thing that remained paramount in Jesse's mind at the moment was Karen.

What the hell was wrong with him? A beautiful woman had just unquestionably issued a sexual invitation to him, and he'd walked away. Why hadn't he taken advantage of what she'd offered him?

He'd excused it at the moment with the need to get the truth about Paul out into the open before their relationship took such an important step. But in his heart, Jesse knew it was more than that. It was his innate fear of allowing anyone behind the emotional wall he'd built around himself.

Why couldn't he open himself to other people? Had he inherited more than his eye color from his father? Iris had often said that both Diane's and Emily's fun-loving, easy-going ways mirrored their mother's, Frank Kingston's first wife. Jesse's mother, the second Mrs. Frank Kingston, had been the total opposite of Jesse, warm and outgoing. Much like Karen. That left only Frank from whom Jesse could have inherited his personality. A sad inheritance indeed.

From the time his mother had died, Jesse had felt betrayed by her death. That betrayal had turned his outlook on life a bit cynical, and cynicism had helped reinforce the wall he'd built around his emotions. Until now, even though his mother had left his father when Jesse was a baby, he hadn't realized how much of his emotional defenses had been dictated by Frank Kingston after he returned to his father's house.

Jesse could still smell the odor of the cigarette smoke that had haloed Frank the day he'd stood before his father's *throne* for the first time. Frank had coldly glared at the quaking nine-year-old from beneath lowered black eyebrows. Jesse had been scared, alone and unsure why this man harbored such anger for his only male child. He'd done nothing except come to his father's house as the courts had instructed. This was not the laughing, loving man his mother had told him about. Just one more way in which she'd betrayed him.

There had been no welcome on that first day. His father had simply recited the rules of the house and the punishment for any infraction. He'd told Jesse where his room was, then curtly dismissed him. The only other times he'd paid Jesse any attention was when he'd summoned him to come before him for punishments.

But that was okay with Jesse. Even his raucous, fun-loving stepsisters and the Kingston's loving housekeeper hadn't been a strong enough buffer to protect Jesse's tender feelings from this austere, stoic man who was his father. He'd done his chores and, when things got rough, he'd run into the solitude of the forest, and in one way or another, he'd been running from life ever since.

It had been easy for him to hold Frank, Diane, and Emily at arm's length, but Karen was another matter altogether. He didn't want Karen at a distance. But how close could he let her come and still protect his own heart?

That question brought him upright in bed to stare into the darkness. His heart? Was he falling in love with her?

Chapter 9

Karen rolled to her side, then to the other side. The blankets and sheet tangled around her legs. Finally, she gave up. Propping the pillow against the bed's headboard, she leaned against it, pulled the bed linens up to her chest, and stared into the darkness.

She'd been attempting, without success, to forget what had happened in the living room. Every time she tried to push it from her head, and she thought she'd been successful, it popped right back. Maybe she should just give up the fight and think about it, clear it out of her head once and for all, and then possibly find the oblivion she sought in sleep. Sighing, she allowed the questions admittance.

What is Jesse's problem? Why had he pushed her away? In her gut, she knew it wasn't just her. *It's everyone: his friends, his family, anyone that might break through his emotional shell.* Every time someone got close or even the suggestion of them getting close to him arose, he backed off. But that didn't make his rejection of her any less painful, less humiliating. Bottom line? She'd opened herself to him, and he'd not only rejected her, he'd closed himself off from her. She wasn't sure which hurt more.

Paul had been distant, but not like this. They'd been able to have a relationship, to candidly express their emotions to each other, even if that relationship hadn't been as open as she would have liked.

Jesse couldn't seem to even allow that much to happen. Did she want to get involved with another man who couldn't share himself with her?

The answer rang through her mind, loud and clear. After a few months of grieving, she'd been able to let go of Paul, but no matter how hard she tried, she knew she could not let go of Jesse. In the short time she'd known him, he'd become a big part of her life and a very important part, a part she wanted to keep there—permanently.

Jesse Kingston was a puzzle. That was a given. However, having passed many hours doing anagrams while her sister paraded before a panel of beauty pageant judges, Karen had become quite adept at solving puzzles. She vowed to break through the barrier Jesse had put up. There was too much at stake not to.

Laying her hand over the slight swelling below her waist, she finally admitted to something she'd known for a while. She and Paul had never shared the deep love that sustains a relationship through the years. Jesse, on the other hand, stirred things deep inside her. In her heart it wasn't a father for her child she wanted as much as it was something Paul had never been able to give her—the other half of her soul.

When Karen walked into the kitchen the following morning, she had to admit, after seeing her drawn face in the bathroom mirror, that Jesse didn't look much better than she did. At least he hadn't gone to bed, dismissed her, and gotten a good night's sleep. Maybe her bruised ego needed to know that he hadn't been able to forget their encounter any more than she had. Whatever the reason, she found his pallor satisfying.

She poured herself a cup of coffee, added cream and sugar, and took a seat across from him at the table. Sipping her coffee, she gazed at him over the lip of her cup. He didn't meet her gaze. Instead, he concentrated on something outside the window.

Screwing up her courage, she addressed the thing that hovered between them like an avenging angel. "So, I take it that you've decided to totally ignore what happened last night."

Jesse kept his gaze turned from her. "Don't you mean what didn't happen?" His low voice made it seem as if he was speaking to himself.

Karen shrugged. "Semantics." She would not be deterred. "But have it your way, what didn't happen." After setting her cup down, she leaned her elbows on the table and folded her hands. "Either way, it's not going to go away."

Still not meeting her gaze, he stood and went to the counter to refill his cup. "And talking about it isn't going to make it go away either."

For a second Karen felt like she was face-to-face again with that arrogant man she'd first met in the diner. Back then, he'd intimated her into silence, but not now, not when she knew this attitude he'd adopted was part of the wall he threw up between himself and anyone daring to delve into the real Jesse Kingston.

"We need to talk about this. It's not going away, and we can't run from it."

Jesse turned to face her. She was right, and he was willing. If he hadn't learned anything else from all that introspection last night, he'd found that he did not want Karen to walk out of his life and that, if necessary and unless he felt it would hurt her in some way, he'd put up a damned hard fight to keep that from happening.

"And we will talk, I promise. But this is not the time." When she shook her head, he continued. "Karen, please believe me when I say I'm not trying to avoid talking about last night. Right now, we need to get on the road." He sighed. "I found out more about the fire scene last night, and called your sister this morning to tell her. We need to meet Elle up there as soon as we can."

His statement seemed to change Karen's dogged focus from him to the mystery of Paul's death. But he could tell by the determined set of her mouth that this didn't mean she'd given up. She'd just shelved the discussion of the previous night . . . for the moment.

"What did you find out?"

Jesse came back to the table. He told her about Butch Haskell's phone call. "He seems to think the dent we found was made by a chopper."

"What's so unusual about that? Don't they use helicopters to carry water to the fires?"

He nodded. "The problem is, we didn't have any up in that area that day. I want to stop at Dave's on the way up the mountain to see if he heard anything that day." He finished his coffee, put the cup in the sink and held out his hand to her. "Let's go."

Dave met them in his yard and walked to the side of the car. He leaned in the open window, and his face broke into a welcoming smile at the sight of Karen.

"Hello, little lady. I see he hasn't chased you away yet." He threw Jesse a look that said he was glad he'd taken his advice, at least for now, and hung on to Karen.

Karen smiled and glanced at Jesse. "Not for lack of trying, Dave." Jesse immediately thought of the previous night and inwardly cringed. She winked at the old man. "But I'm not that easy to chase off."

Jesse sighed under his breath. He surprised himself by thinking, *Thank goodness.*

"Good for you." Dave turned to Jesse and slapped him on the shoulder. "Appears to me that she's got you pegged, my boy. I'd just roll over and surrender."

Neither of them had any idea how much Jesse wanted to do just that, but there were things, important things standing in the way. Until he'd removed them, he had no choice but to keep his emotional distance.

Glancing at Karen, he noted the pink rising in her cheeks. "Put a sock in it, old man," Jesse said, forcing a laugh. "You're embarrassing the lady." Before Dave could reply, Jesse pushed on. "We stopped by to ask you a question."

"Ask away. If I can answer you, I will."

"The day Paul died in the fire, did you hear any choppers overhead?"

An impatient sigh issued from Dave. "I thought you were giving this up."

That came as no surprise. After the conversation they'd had in the truck, Jesse would have been shocked if Dave hadn't said anything.

Jesse held Dave's gaze. "Not until I have answers. Did you hear a chopper?"

Dave shook his head. "No. And I would have if there had been any. Seems like no matter where they're going, they usually fly right over my cabin and shake the damned windows."

Jesse frowned.

Karen leaned around Jesse for a better view of Dave. "You're sure?"

"Little lady, I'm as sure as I am that the sun will come up tomorrow, but if you doubt me, your boyfriend here is a ranger. If they were flying choppers into that fire, wouldn't he have known?"

Before the *boyfriend* remark could launch this conversation in a direction Jesse didn't want to go, he started the car. "Thanks, Dave. We gotta run. Have a good day."

"Stop back on your way off the mountain. I'll put on the coffee pot." He smiled broadly at them, then, as Jesse threw the car in reverse, stepped away.

"We'll probably be coming down by the north road. But thanks anyway."

They were almost to the burn site when Karen finally voiced the conclusion she'd come to after much thought. "Maybe there was a chopper, and it just didn't fly over Dave's cabin. Maybe it came in from a different direction."

"Maybe," was all Jesse said, but the frown lines in his forehead told her he had been as busy sorting out what Dave had said as she'd been. "There's a small lake on the other side of the ridge where they could have used their water buckets to scoop water. The return route would have missed Dave's cabin." He sighed. "The only problem with our theories is that Butch checked and no helicopters were dispatched by the Preserve for that fire."

Karen fell silent for a few moments. "If no copters were dispatched, then maybe Butch was wrong about the indentation

Elle found. Maybe that mark wasn't from a helicopter. Maybe it was from something else? After all, Butch didn't actually see it. He's only going by what he overheard Elle tell Hank."

Jesse pulled the car into the lot beside Karen's red sports car. Elle and Scott were sitting on one of the split-rail fences bordering the parking area. "I guess we'll see. According to Butch, if it was a chopper, then there should be a mark from the other landing skid running parallel to the one Elle found." He turned off the car. "And the only way we'll find that out is to go look."

"I borrowed those from the State Troopers' evidence lab this morning, just in case I missed something the other day." Elle pointed at several silver paint cans sitting beside the blackened stump of a tree. "Give me a hand with them, Karen."

Glaring sunlight filtered through the skeletal remains of the trees and glinted off the shiny metal, lending a bit of brightness to an otherwise macabre scene. The hot day and the unusually high humidity enhanced the smell of burned wood that still lingered over the area.

Karen picked up two of the canisters and followed Elle toward a particularly black spot on the forest floor. Elle removed her fold-up shovel from her evidence case. Using the tip, she moved the earth around, as though searching for something.

"So, have you told him yet?" Elle asked, her voice just loud enough not to carry to where Scott and Jesse stood talking, her gaze going pointedly to Karen's stomach.

"Yes, last night."

"How did he take it?" Elle moved away from the blackened area and toward where she'd found the indentation the day before.

Karen followed. "All right, I guess."

Elle straightened, her forehead knitted in a frown. "You guess? Don't you know?"

"Well, after I told him, he seemed angry, but later he said he wasn't. He said he was just shocked, then he tried to tell me why, but I . . . we . . . ." She looked at her feet, hoping Elle wouldn't see the color she felt rising to her cheeks.

She was trying to find the words to tell Elle what had happened on the couch, but before she could, a gasp burst from Elle. "I'll be damned."

Thankful for whatever had distracted Elle, Karen moved to her side. After all, how do you tell your sister you'd tried to seduce a man, and he turned you down? She looked down at where Elle had pushed aside the grass and uncovered another track, identical to the one they'd found the day before.

"Jesse. Scott. Take a look at this." Elle spread the grass farther to more fully disclose the track.

Scott and Jesse hurried over.

"The other track," Jesse said under his breath.

"We can't jump to any conclusions until we take some measurements," Elle cautioned. "My Air-Medi friend sent me the specs for a small copter. He said it would need about fifty square feet to land and," she glanced around, "this clearing is more than adequate for that." She turned to her husband. "Scott, hand me my measuring tape from that case."

Scott quickly did as she asked.

"Jesse, hold the grass back from that other indentation." When Jesse had obliged, she stretched the tape between the marks, noted the length, and again turned to Scott. "Snap a picture of this." After the camera clicked, Elle laid the tape along the length of the mark and recorded the measurements. "Again," she instructed, holding the tape in place. The camera clicked again.

From the pocket of her jeans, Elle pulled a folded sheet of paper. Opening it, she checked her measurements against the figures on the paper.

"What the hell's going on here?"

A strident voice broke through their concentration. They all spun in the direction of the voice. Karen's heart pounded.

Glaring at Elle, Hank Thompson tromped toward them. "I thought I told you to stay away from here." Then, before Elle could say anything, he charged at Jesse, stopping when he was inches from him, their noses almost touching. "And I told you to go home and not to nose around up here trying to solve a case that's already been solved. I should fire your ass right on the spot. The only reason I'm not going to is because you're one of my best rangers. But don't push me, Kingston."

Jesse stepped back from his raging boss and returned his angry glare. "What is it, Hank? Are you afraid we'll find something you don't want found?"

Hank's face grew red with suppressed anger. "What the hell is that supposed to mean?"

"It means you've been trying your damndest to keep us away from here. That tends to make a reasonable person wonder why."

Karen could have sworn that Hank's face took on a purple hue. Jesse stiffened. She grabbed Jesse's arm in an effort to forestall anything he may have on his mind that could land him in jail for assault.

"This place is off limits to the public," Hank ground out between clenched teeth.

Jesse glanced around them. "I don't see any signs."

The desire to do Jesse bodily harm glowed plainly in Hank's eyes. Fear rose up to choke Karen. Terror clutched her heart in a stranglehold .

She tightened her fingers around Jesse's arm. "Don't push him."

Jesse covered her hand with his and gave it a reassuring squeeze. Elle and Scott moved closer to Jesse, as if to protect him. Hank glared at each of them in turn.

"The signs will go up this afternoon. After that, if I catch any of you here, I'll have you arrested for trespassing."

"You better hope you're not the one who lands in jail." Jesse flashed that cynical smile that Karen new so well.

"Threatening me can have dire consequences." Hank wagged his finger under Jesse's nose. "You better buy a newspaper, Kingston, and check the classifieds because as of now, you're unemployed." Hank turned on his heel and strode away.

Rather than leave, Hank sat in his car and watched as they all packed up and drove away.

Chapter 10

Karen had been staring silently out the car's windshield for the last three miles of their descent off the mountain. No matter what he'd done to engage her in conversation, she hadn't responded.

"Are you ever going to speak to me again?" Jesse asked as he pulled the car to a stop beside the road.

She turned on him, her face furious. "Couldn't you have talked to him nicely so he didn't get mad?'

There was no need to explain who she was referring to. Hank Thompson. Jesse shrugged. He felt totally justified in his anger at Hank. "I suppose I could have. But what difference would it have made?"

Karen tossed her hair back over her shoulder. The abruptness of the motion transmitted clearly the depth of her anger. She kept her face turned away from him.

"Well, he might not have fired you." She paused and bit her quivering bottom lip. "And . . . oh, God, he was so angry. He was so . . . so angry. He could have—"

"What?"

For the first time since he'd stopped the car, she stared directly at him. Moisture filled her eyes. She blinked and tears streamed down her cheeks like raindrops on a window pane. She seemed not to notice them.

"He could have hurt you."

The pain reflected in her eyes made his heart twist painfully in his chest. "But he didn't hurt me." He took her by the shoulders and looked deep into her swimming eyes. "And would that have mattered to you?"

She dipped her head, then raised it and looked him in the eyes.

"Very much." Her raspy voice was barely audible. Her sweet breath fanned his cheeks, sending his blood racing around his body.

Jesse breathed deeply. He had to know. "Why, Karen? Why would it matter?"

Cupping the sides of his face in her hands, she swallowed hard. "Because I can't lose someone else that I . . . care about."

Care was not exactly the word he'd hoped to hear. But he'd take it, for now. He pulled her to him and held her for a long time. Finally, he pressed his lips against her forehead and whispered, "I'm sorry. I didn't mean to scare you."

Karen raised her face to look at him. "I know. It's just that . . . ." Her bottom lip quivered.

Jesse caught his breath. Since before his mother had died, no one had shed tears for him. No one had cared enough about him to worry about his safety. With a jolt, he realized that wasn't true. Iris, Emily, and Diane had cared, and he'd repaid their concern with indifference and coldness because he'd been too busy reinforcing that protective shield around his emotions.

Was he making the same mistake with Karen? But did he dare to commit to more, to something with a lot more longevity? He pushed that thought aside. What he needed to do now was get Karen's fears in hand, give her back the peace the argument with Hank had stolen from her.

From the corner of her eye Karen saw him open the car door, get out, then lean over the seat. He extracted something from the back seat, then closed the door. Suddenly, he appeared outside her window. The door opened, and he took her hand.

"Come on. I want to show you something."

Karen noted a rolled up blanket under his arm. Hesitantly, she took his hand. As his fingers closed over hers, tingles danced up her arm. His warm flesh pressing hers sent a wave of reassurance through her and helped dispel the fear that had festered inside her since his confrontation with Hank. Feeling better, she slipped from the car and then followed him down a worn path that lead into a grove of towering, majestic pine trees sitting atop a cliff overlooking an expanse of valley that took her breath away.

A soft breeze carried with it the fragrance of pine. A thick bed of pine needles muffled their footsteps. The vividly blue sky beyond the canopy of trees nearly blinded her. Birds sang all around them. Contentment surrounded her and flooded through her like hot chocolate before a warm fire on a cold night.

They'd gone several hundred yards when Jesse stopped, released her hand, and then spread the blanket on the pine needles. From the clearing in which she stood, Karen had a panoramic view of the valley below them. Mountains rose to touch the heavens and then dipped into verdant valleys. Long shadows spread dark fingers over the landscape as though protecting the peace of the setting.

"It's beautiful," she whispered afraid to disturb the serenity of the place if she spoke too loudly.

"It's where I come when I need to think." Jesse took her hand and stood beside her, gazing out over the valley.

Had he shared this with anyone else? She hoped not. The idea of him thinking of her as special enough to share his secret haven helped dispel the last of the fear to which Hank's tirade had given birth.

"I can understand why. It's so quiet. You can almost hear the earth's breath." Then she turned her face away and laughed at her foolish statement.

He caught her chin in his hand and gently turned her to look at him. With his free hand, he swept the hair back from her forehead, then let his fingers trail down her neck.

Karen tried to read his thoughts. What she saw in his expression sent shivers coursing through her. "Jesse . . . ."

The husky sound of his name on her lips shot a wave of heat through Jesse, heat so strong he had to fight for breath. Lord, but she was so lovely, so sweet, so tantalizing. He knew that he could easily get lost in Karen and never find his way out. Despite that, he wanted her, and this time he shut out the warnings from his conscience and went with his gut.

"Karen?" He had no idea if she understood what he was asking for, but her smile told him he needn't have worried.

She raised herself on tiptoe, putting her mouth within a hair's breadth of his. "Kiss me, Jesse Kingston."

He stroked her cheek. The ghosts of the tears she'd shed for him still lingered on her face. He kissed each one, letting his lips linger against her creamy skin, tasting the salt and conveying with his touch how much he regretted scaring her.

Her skin reminded him of rich satin, smooth, silky and cooled by the wind. His head grew light. Touching Karen was like falling into one of the wildfires he'd fought on the mountain. But instead of running away, he was being consumed by a heat that drove him to want more. He shifted her slightly so her body aligned perfectly with his, making his need known by the pressure of his groan against her stomach. Her moan started deep inside her and found its way to the surface, igniting his already-smoldering need.

Slowly he lowered his mouth to hers. At the first touch of flesh on flesh, the painful intensity of life surging back into him, the first he'd felt since before Paul's death, almost made him cry out. He was suddenly aware of every pore in his body, every breath wrenched from his lungs, every ounce of blood rushing through his veins.

He wanted Karen as much as he wanted to see the next sunrise. With one deft movement, he lowered her to the blanket and then pressed her backwards, half covering her body with his. She stiffened beneath him.

He paused. What if he'd read her wrong? What if this was not what she wanted? "Now is the time to stop me," he murmured.

Karen ran her fingertip over his lips. "Do I look like a woman who wants to stop you?"

Jesse stared down at her. Beneath her half closed lids, desire filled her eyes. Her lips parted slightly in invitation. Light pink tinted her cheeks. The flowery scent of her intoxicating perfume drifted up to him.

His groin hardened painfully. He opened his mouth to speak. She smiled the smile of a wanton and slipped her fingertip inside his bottom lip to caress the sensitive inner skin.

He gasped and ran his hand over her breast and down to her waist. Feeling the very slight swelling there, he hesitated.

"The baby?"

"The baby will be fine," she whispered back and drew his mouth back to hers.

Her tongue slipped between his parted lips. Tingles of pleasure danced up Jesse's spine. She was seducing him, and he was a more than willing victim. Even if he'd wanted to escape, he couldn't.

He pulled back and levered himself to a kneeling position. Slowly, never breaking eye contact, he slipped the buttons on her blouse free and then folded the edges back. Beneath the material, a lacy bra cupped two very delicate breasts. He'd never been particularly drawn to women with large breasts so Karen's made him smile in anticipation of unveiling them.

He ran the tip of his finger over the exposed flesh above the lace. Karen closed her eyes and moaned. The sound pierced him like a hot poker.

Jesse barely remembered taking off her blouse and bra. All he knew was now, from the waist up, she lay gloriously naked before him. Gently, he touched her, kneaded the soft flesh in his hot palms and felt the tips harden in response to his caress. Her unfettered moans reverberated around the small clearing, rousing birds from the trees. Afraid they'd be overheard, Jesse silenced her with his mouth.

The kiss seemed to instantly catch fire and then rage out of control. Karen squirmed beneath him, arching her body, silently begging for his touch, and at the same time, clawing at his clothes.

His mind went blank and the next thing he knew his clothes and the remainder of Karen's were gone, and the searing heat of her naked flesh was pressing against him. Biting down hard on his lip, he fought not to rush her. But she wasn't about to wait.

Karen felt as if her head would explode with the blood pounding through it. Her entire body had come alive in a way that seemed almost painful, yet intensely pleasurable. Each breath of breeze, each pine needle below them, each brush of Jesse's lips across her naked skin was magnified far beyond anything she thought she could sanely tolerate.

Yet, she did. Barely. Passion this strong was something she'd never experienced before. She couldn't seem to get enough of touching Jesse and having him touch her. Yet she still hungered for more, much more.

Then Jesse slid his fingers over the apex of her thighs and into the warmth between them. As though an unseen hand clutched her lungs, paralyzing them, she stopped breathing.

Feel! Feel! she told herself. And she did. Every callous on his gentle hands. Every abrasive brush of them against her overly-sensitized skin. She pressed herself harder against him, silently begging him for more.

Still he held back from giving her what she needed most—him—inside her.

"Jesse" The raspy voice uttering his name fell on her ears as that of a stranger, yet she knew it was her own.

Of their own free will, her hips thrust up to him, grinding against him. He moved over her, his gaze locked with hers. Just before he filled her, Jesse gasped her name. Then the world faded into a blur of unbridled motion and searing passion that built and expanded until it exploded in a shower of white lights. Again, he gasped her name, stiffened and then collapsed on top of her.

Breath tore from his chest. His lungs were on fire. A description of how a fellow ranger had felt after making love to a woman passed through Jesse's mind. He'd said the earth moved. At the time, Jesse had thought it ridiculous, but now . . . .

Never in his life had Jesse experienced anything like what had just happened with Karen. There could only be one explanation for the difference between every other women with whom he'd had raw sex, and this mind-blowing experience with Karen.

He was in love with her.

The only problem was, how, when he didn't even love himself, could he love Karen completely as she deserved to be loved?

"We better get dressed," Jesse said, when he'd regained his ability to speak.

He rose from the blanket, gathered Karen's clothes and handed them to her. Turning his back, partially to give her some privacy, but partially because he couldn't make eye contact with her without pouring out what filled his heart to overflowing, he picked up his own clothing and began putting them on.

He didn't hate what he'd done or regret one moment of their time together. He'd loved every second of making love to Karen. What did bother him was what the act signified—a promise of commitment.

With the exception of his mother, Jesse had carefully steered clear of commitment and putting his heart out there to be stomped on. He wasn't even totally sure yet that what he felt for Karen was the everlasting, till-death-us-do-part kind of love.

The very last thing he wanted to do was hurt Karen any more than she had been, any more than she would be when he told her about Paul. And there was only one way to prevent that. He'd hold on to his secret about Paul, a secret that would serve no purpose to reveal now, help her find out how Paul died, put her in her car, and send her back to the city.

"Jesse." She'd come up behind him and snaked her arms around his waist.

Biting his lip, it took all the strength Jesse could muster to pull free of her embrace. He stooped to pick up the blanket, shook the pine needles off, and then began to fold it. "It's getting late. We should get out of here before it gets dark."

From the corner of his eye, he could see the stricken expression on her face. Hatred for himself boiled up in him. But he held his tongue and his resolve.

"Jesse? Are you sorry we made love?"

Before he could answer, a loud *crack* and the sound of something hitting the trunk of the tree beside them rang out. Chips of bark flew into the air, hitting Karen in the cheek. Shocked registered on her face. She cried out and clutched her cheek.

Jesse grabbed her and threw her to the ground, covering her with his body. She struggled to free herself but his hold was relentless.

"Stay down. Someone's shooting at us."

Chapter 11

The fear Karen had experienced when Hank and Jesse had confronted each other earlier was nothing in comparison to the terror holding her in its icy grip now. Her cheek stung where the bark had hit her, and the sensation of warm liquid trickling down her face told her she'd probably been cut. Another fear gripped her.

"Jesse, are you—"

"Shh. I'm fine." His whispered words brushed her cheek.

For what seemed like hours, they laid motionless, waiting, listening for footsteps that would tell them their assailant was coming to check the results of his work. Jesse lay sprawled over Karen, shielding her from the unknown. Her labored breath brushed his face. Her body trembled beneath him. Her rapid heartbeat reverberated against his chest, keeping time with his own.

After what seemed an eternity and no more shots were fired, Jesse levered himself off her, but stayed low. When she made to rise, too, he pushed her back. "No, stay down. I'm going to see if whoever shot at us is still there."

Before he could move, Karen snaked her arms around his neck and hauled him back down on top of her, preventing him from going anywhere. "No!"

"Karen—"

"No." She tightened her hold. "You don't have a gun. What if he's still there and he comes after you? Let's get back to the car and call the police on my cell phone. Let them take care of it." Her fingers dug into his neck. "Please, Jesse."

He dipped his head in indecision for a moment. While

everything in him said to find the bastard that had shot at them and wring his neck like a scrawny chicken, common sense told him to think of Karen first. He looked into her fear-filled face. He couldn't stand seeing her like this. He had to get her to somewhere where she'd be safe.

"Okay." Still crouching low, he got to his feet. "Stay down."

Karen did as he instructed, all the while clinging to his presence like a drowning man. On their hands and knees they crawled to the shelter of a large boulder outcropping. Jesse pulled her to him, and they rested their backs against the cool stone. Through the thick brush, Karen could just make out the car parked beside the road.

"We have a straight shot to the car from here. Stay low and keep behind the bushes." He grabbed her hand, and they slipped into the cover of a heavy growth of mountain laurel. Moments later he wrenched open the car door and shoved her inside. "Get on the floor," he commanded in a don't-argue-with-me voice, then disappeared around the back bumper.

Karen did as he'd told her. Curling herself into a tight ball on the car's floorboard, she hugged her stomach, her one thought, to guard her unborn child against harm. Her fingers curled into her palms. The pain of her nails biting into her flesh helped her focus, in a strange way.

Moments later the driver's door opened, and Jesse scrambled into the seat.

From above she could hear the jingle of metal as Jesse fumbled with the key in the ignition. Karen closed her eyes and waited for another shot to ring out, but none came. The engine roared to life. Jesse threw the car into drive and stomped down on the gas pedal. As the car lurched forward, a spray of gravel flew into the air.

The car fishtailed, then bumped and jostled over the dirt road. When she detected the smoothness of paved road beneath the tires, she opened her eyes. Overhead, trees and sky whizzed by as the car hurtled down the mountain toward the main road. She let out a long held breath and slowly pulled herself up and into the passenger seat.

"Who would shoot at us?" Her quavering voice reflected the residual terror that still churned sickeningly inside her.

When Jesse didn't answer, she turned to him. Gaze locked on the road, his tightly clenched jaw muscles vibrated against his cheek. His white-knuckled hands gripped the steering wheel with a frightening strength and matched the pallor of his complexion.

"Well, there's only one person who has worked endlessly to keep us away from that burn site and finding out the truth surrounding Paul's death." Jesse slowed the car to a safer speed, then glanced at her. "What's your guess?"

Karen sucked in her breath. *He couldn't possibly mean . . . .* "Hank? You think Hank shot at us? Just because he's mad at you?"

"It's a lot more than just being mad at me, Karen. Think about it. He's done all he could to keep us away from there. He sent me home to stop me from asking questions. He had the place declared off limits by the Conservation Department." Jesse laughed derisively. "He even fired me. I'm open to suggestions here, Karen, but if he's not hiding something, then what the hell is he doing?"

Karen had no answer. Silently, she dug in her purse, pulled out her cell phone and waited for the dispatcher to answer her 911 call. Too nervous to relay the happenings in the woods, she handed the phone to Jesse and listened while he related what had been one of the most frightening incidents of her life.

Jesse disconnected the call, and gave the phone to Karen. "I have to go back and meet the police to show them where we were. I don't want you alone at the house. I'm going to drop you off at the motel to stay with Elle."

Karen just nodded. He could tell by her silence and the way she was clutching her hands in her lap that she was still shaken by what they'd been through and had no desire to go back there. At least he hoped that was the case.

He laid his hand on hers. They were cold and stiff. "Karen, you're safe now. You can stay with Elle until I get done on the mountain. I'll come back for you as soon as it's over."

She shook her head. "No. I'll have Elle bring me back to your house."

"But—"

She held up her hand to stop him. "Jesse, a lot has happened in the last few hours. I need time to think."

Think. What about? That they'd been shot at or that he'd walked away from her after they'd shared something so beautiful it still had the power to weaken his knees just thinking about it?

Jesse removed his hand from hers. "Think about what? The gunshot or what's happening between us?"

Karen paused before answering him. Aside from the trauma of being shot at, ever since he'd turned his back on her after they made love, serious doubts had been accosting her about Jesse. Was she expecting more from him than he could give?

Since she'd met him, her priorities had gotten all screwed up. By concentrating on finding the man Jesse kept hidden somewhere deep inside, she'd put her baby's happiness on hold. She'd become sidetracked from her original purpose for coming to Bristol and seeking out this man.

Since Jesse obviously didn't seem interested in any long-term relationship, it was time she got her head on straight and put her priorities back in place. And priority number one was finding Paul's family. Let Jesse chase the bad guys. She shouldn't be putting herself or her child at risk playing detective.

"Yes, there is something happening between us, and we need to talk about it. But first, I need to start thinking about . . . " she placed her hand on her stomach. "My baby." She turned toward him. "I never told you the other reason I came here."

"I thought you came here to find out what really happened to Paul." Jesse glanced at her, then back to the road.

She took a deep breath, then plunged on. "There was that. But it wasn't just to find out what happened to Paul." She swallowed hard, trying to work up the courage to get it all up front once and for all. "I want to know how to find Paul's family. I want my child to know them, and I need you to help me do that."

The silence that engulfed the interior of the car was deafening.

Elle opened the motel room door at the first knock. "Karen—" Whatever the rest of the greeting was that Elle had been about to voice, stopped abruptly. Elle stared at her sister. "What happened to your face?"

Karen scanned the small, clean, utilitarian motel room. The night table and the table under the window held neatly piled Styrofoam cups and discarded food wrappers. The smell of stale coffee and French fries hung in the air. "Where's Scott?"

"He went to find a store to buy me crackers." Elle rubbed her flat stomach. "Every other woman gets morning sickness. I get afternoon sickness."

Preoccupied by the day's events, Karen barely heard what Elle said. "Oh."

Frowning, Elle took Karen's arm and guided her into the room and onto the foot of the bed. "What happened to your face?"

"We were shot at."

Elle's mouth fell open. "Oh, my God! By who?"

Karen shook her head. "No idea. Or at least none with any solid proof. Jesse thinks it may have been Hank. He just went up there with the police to look around." Karen put her hand to her stinging cheek. "I got hit with flying bark."

The gesture pushed Elle into action. "Let me look at that cut." Elle went to the bathroom and returned with a wet washcloth and began swabbing at Karen's bloody cheek. "It's just a scratch." She laid the cloth aside, dried the skin and applied antiseptic cream and a small bandage, then sat down to stare at Karen.

When Elle remained silent, Karen prodded her. "What?"

"There's something I have to tell you." Taking a seat at the small table under the window, Elle crossed her legs. "When Scott and I left the burn site, we decide to go have a talk with Hank, and see if we could find out why he was so adamant about all of us staying away from the burn site. He wasn't in his office, so his assistant told us where he lived."

"And?" Karen was growing impatient with what seemed to be developing into a long, drawn-out story.

"I don't know how much this means, but, Karen, have you ever seen Hank's house?"

Karen shook her head.

Elle rolled her eyes. "It's the most gorgeous log house I've ever seen. Three stories. Decks all around. Cathedral ceilings. A fireplace big enough to hold a party in. Scott guessed the square footage at about four thousand. Far beyond anything I'd think Hank could afford on his salary. And that's not all. His wife answered the door, and the clothes she was wearing didn't come from any rack I could afford to shop from." She edged forward on her chair. "Karen, they must have another income."

Confusion overwhelmed Karen. "I don't understand what this has to do with Paul."

"Neither do I," Elle said, "but I'm going to find out." She cleared her throat and hesitated before going on. "Scott says if it was in Florida, he'd think drugs."

Karen was stunned. Of all the things she'd guessed to be the cause of Paul's death, drugs had never entered her mind.

"That's not all," Elle went on. "I got the results back from the lab today on those soil samples we took at the burn site. They found gasoline. That means someone poured gas over that site to make it burn hotter than it already was." She covered Karen's hand with hers. "Scott agrees with me that the addition to the already burning fire may have been used to cover something more sinister that involved Paul." She paused again. "Karen, whoever poured that gas on the fire wanted him silenced for good."

From the hesitation in her voice and the look on her face, Karen knew there was more that Elle hadn't said. So she put her sister's thoughts into words. "Or he was part of it, and they decided that Paul was a liability they didn't need." She waited for Elle to dispute it, but she averted her gaze.

Instantly, Karen recalled for the thousandth time how secretive Paul had been about his life. Were Elle's suspicions right?

"Is Karen okay?" Emily's concerned voice conveyed the fear written clearly on her face.

Jesse nodded. When he'd asked Em to go with him to the garage to pick up his car and drive hers back, she'd read his troubled face, and he'd had no choice but to tell his sister the story of the day's events—most of them. What happened before the shot was fired remained between him and Karen.

"She's fine. Shaken, but not hurt except for a scratch on her cheek where she was hit by flying bark." He lifted his coffee cup to his mouth, took a sip, made a face and then set the cup down. "You still make lousy coffee."

"Forget my coffee making skills. Where's Karen?"

He pushed the cup away from him. "She's with Elle at the motel."

"Jesse, who do you think shot at you?"

Jesse told her about the previous attempts on their lives, the break-in at Karen's' room and his run-in with Hank earlier that day. "It makes sense that it was him, but I don't have any proof. The police didn't find any shell casings or footprints." He stood and went to stare out the kitchen window toward his house. "I was going to wait until we had the mystery of Paul's death solved, but with all that's happened, I can't afford to wait. I'm going to encourage Karen to go back to the city."

For a few seconds, Emily remained thoughtfully silent. "I don't think she'll go."

Jesse swung toward her. "She has to. It's not safe for her here."

"That doesn't mean she'll go." Emily's laughter rippled around the room. "It's amazing how blind you men can be." She went to stand beside him. "Jesse, a blind man can see she's in love with you, and she's not going to leave you." She tilted her head to see his face better. "And unless I miss my guess, you're in love with her, too."

He saw no sense in denying Emily statement. Why bother? If he had his way, Karen would be gone soon. "All the more reason for her to leave. If this nut case trying to stop us doesn't hurt her, then I will." Jesse didn't want to look at Emily and see the condemnation in her eyes.

"Why would you hurt her?"

Jesse laughed derisively. "I'm my father's son. We all know that, Em."

"Well, I seem to be out of the information loop then, because I know no such thing." She laid her hand on his arm.

She had no idea what she was talking about. Jesse ripped away from her grip and went back to the table. "I don't want to talk about this."

Determinedly, Emily followed him. "Well, maybe it's time you did."

She sat and leaned forward, forearms on the table top, silently announcing that she was here for the duration and short of him walking out, she was not about to drop the subject. Oddly, he made no move to leave.

"You're right about one thing, you are like our father."

Jesse hadn't seen that coming. His head shot up, and he stared at her. "Well, I'm glad at least you see that."

"You're like he was *before* life kicked him in the head and turned him into a cynical old man with his heart encased in stone. You were too young to remember him like that, but Diane and I remember a fun-loving man who played games with us, handed out hugs like candy and laughed at our silly jokes." She took a deep breath before going on. "I'm sorry you never knew that man.

"Then he met your mom, married her, and brought her here to live. From the first, we knew she hated this rural life. She was a city girl. Cows, horses, and all that this life encompassed just smothered her until she had to get away." Tentatively, she touched his arm, but his time he didn't pull away. "Jesse, when your mom left him, it broke his heart. Diane and I spent many nights listening to him cry. Then one day, the tears stopped. He put his heart in cold storage and became the man you met when you came here to live."

Despite Emily's sincerity, Jesse was having a lot of difficulty picturing either the fun-loving father she'd described, or the stoic, emotionless man he'd known ever being the type that would cry over the loss of a woman.

Anger that had been boiling inside Jesse for years broke through. "This doesn't change anything, Em. I was his son, and he treated me worse than a stepchild."

"Yes, he did. But that doesn't make you anything like him."

He laughed without humor. "What does it make me then?"

"Someone who's had his love thrown in his face and as a result, locked his emotions away to protect himself."

Her words hit a raw spot in Jesse, a wound that had never healed. He'd already figured out that he'd built a wall around his emotions. His problem was, until he could find a way to claw his way over it, he had no hope of a relationship with Karen or anyone else.

"So, wise one, how do you suggest I fix it?" Sarcasm was easier than letting her know she'd hit very close to home.

"First of all, I know you have love inside you. You care about people. You went to bat for Diane when Dad was forcing her into a marriage we all knew was wrong for her. You're busting your butt trying to find out what happened to your best friend. You want Karen away from here so she doesn't get hurt. Someone incapable of love would never do any of those things." She paused as if giving him time to digest what she'd said.

"You're never going to be able to let that love out until you conquer your apprehension about being hurt," she went on. "Not until you force your way through that fear can you get to the rest of your life. You have to bite the bullet and love freely, unconditionally, without fear, and hope you won't be hurt. Because life doesn't come with guarantees, Jesse. It only comes with a reasonable expectation of happiness and the human ability to find it." She squeezed his arm. "Believe me, it's well worth the risks."

She stood and pulled him to his feet. "Lecture over. Now, get out of here, and go talk to Karen."

Chapter 12

When Karen heard Jesse's car drive up outside his house, she was curled up on the couch, absently watching a re-run of a comedy sitcom. Her heart sped up, but she forced herself to remain still. The front door opened and closed, and his footsteps sounded hollowly on the pine hall floor. She clicked the *off* button on the remote, and the house went silent except for the sound of his car keys clattering against the hall tabletop. More footsteps on the wood floor, then the muffled sound of them approaching across the living room carpet.

"Hi," he said from just behind her shoulder.

She could hear the hesitation in his voice. It only served to reinforce her belief that he regretted what had happened in the woods and was now searching for the words to tell her. Humiliation forced her to speak before he could say anything that would make her heart bleed any more than it already was.

"I've taken advantage of you long enough. Elle is going to call me in a few minutes and let me know if there's a room available at the motel. If there is, I'll be out of here tomorrow."

Jesse came around the sofa and sat down beside her. That he looked surprised made her wonder why. "You don't have to move out. You're welcome here as long as you want to stay."

Karen stared at him. "Am I, Jesse?"

"Of course. What gave you the idea that you wouldn't be?"

The question sounded so innocent, as if he really had no idea what had pushed her to make this decision. Was it possible he didn't realize what he'd done? How could he not know? The only answer was when you don't care about someone, their emotions are as closed to you as a bank vault's door. That he'd been so oblivious to her feelings only intensified the pain his rejection had caused, making the resulting wound more raw, more hurtful.

The desire to discuss her decision was something she didn't want to get into, didn't dare get into. The tears were hovering too close to the surface. She forced them back.

"What gave me that idea is of no importance." She stood, ready to leave the room. "I'm going to bed."

"Karen." He took her arm gently, to stop her. "Please, sit down. We need to talk."

Pleasurable little tingles danced over her skin where has hand grasped her, and she had to fight to keep from throwing herself in his arms. Too emotionally defeated from the day's events to fight both herself and him, she pulled her arm free and, making sure to put the length of the couch between them, she retook her seat.

"I've said all I have to say."

Why was she doing this? Why was she opening herself up to an explanation that could only cause more pain? She knew why. Despite everything, a glimmer of hope flamed to life inside her. Maybe he'd say something to explain his rejection, maybe even declare his love and make everything okay again.

"I have something to say. I don't want you in Bristol. I want you to go back to the city as soon as possible."

The ultimate rejection. Pain shot through her chest, as if her heart had been split wide open. It would have hurt less if he'd plunged a knife into her. Paralyzing numbness claimed her body and her senses.

She almost laughed. How foolish she'd been to believe she could change him.

Jesse watched the play of emotions on Karen's face. What he saw was deep hurt. She thought he was chasing her out of town because of what had happened in the woods.

Needing to soothe away the pain in her face, he leaned toward her, but she pulled back out of range of his touch. Her rejection sent stinging arrows of regret spiraling through him.

"Karen, we've been in danger of dying on a mountain road

from defective brakes; your room was trashed. Today we were shot at. The next time we might not be so lucky. The next time might mean . . . ." The idea of anything happening to her was too painful to think about, much less put into words. "I don't want you in the line of fire again, figuratively or actually. That's why I want you to go back to the city."

"And suppose I refuse?"

Coming to Bristol in the first place gave testimony to her determination, and now, she was about to dig in her heels again. Even if it meant losing her, he could not let her stay here and put herself in danger any longer. He hated to do it, but he'd have to hit her where she was most vulnerable.

"I hope you won't, if not for your sake, then for the baby's."

"Let me worry about the baby." As though getting ready to ward off a blow, she stiffened her spine. "I've been thinking about all this, and I don't think they're after me. I think whoever it is, is after you, and I just happened to be there when the attempts are made."

She thought she had it all figured out, but Jesse knew she'd overlooked one detail. "Then how do you explain your room being trashed?"

Karen had no answer for that. "What did you find when you went back into the woods with the police?"

"Nothing. No casings. No footprints. We still don't know who it is trying to stop us." Jesse closed the distance between them and took her cold hand in his. "Whoever it is thinks you know whatever I know. They searched your room looking for anything that might prove that." He squeezed her hand. "I don't want you to go, but if it means keeping you safe, then that's what you have to do."

His words again brought to life that faint flutter of hope in Karen. Did she mean something to him after all? With him holding her hand and the soft brush of his breath against her cheek, she was having trouble thinking. She pulled away.

Then anger blossomed inside her, sudden and raging. How

dare he dictate to her what she *had* to do? He had walked away. He had dismissed her as if she meant nothing to him. Now all of a sudden he was going to play her concerned protector.

Her simmering rage fueled her courage to face him down. "I'm not going anywhere until we find out what happened to Paul."

Jesse sighed and ran his fingers through his hair, frustration evident in his movements. "Karen—"

"I'm not leaving." She set her lips and raised her chin defiantly.

For a moment he looked as though he would give her an argument, then he stood and paced the room several times before stopping in front of her. "Okay, then don't go to the motel. Stay here with me where I can make sure you're safe."

For a long, hesitant moment she stared at him. Could she do that? Could she be near him and not let her guard down, not succumb to his charm and magnetism, not lay her heart on the chopping block again? Then she remembered he didn't want her.

The questions racing through her mind took a different turn. Could she stay here with him and not end up with her heart broken worse than it was already? No. She just didn't have it in her to be battered around emotionally anymore.

"No. I'm going to the motel with Elle. They'll see that I'm okay."

The phone rang, breaking the thick silence that hung in the room. Jesse answered it.

"Hi, Elle. What?" Pause. "Okay, I'll tell her." Pause. "Yeah, sure. No problem. Bye." He hung up and turned to Karen. "That settles it. Elle said there are no available rooms. You'll have to stay here."

Karen felt like a rat trapped in an emotional cage that had no door, no way to escape.

When Jesse entered the kitchen the following morning and found Karen at the table, he knew he looked like hell. He'd had little or no sleep the night before. Knowing Karen slept right down the hall had pounded at him until he'd finally given up on sleep and tried to read. It wasn't long before that too became a futile endeavor, and he gave in to his troubled thoughts.

Not for the first time, he'd realized that what had happened in the pine woods had been a mistake. Before they'd made love in the woods, he'd only dreamed about holding Karen in his arms and what it would be like to lose himself in her. Now that they'd made love, the images had become like ever-present specters, hovering over him, taunting him with their memory.

Now, seeing her in the flesh, the memories again attacked. Deep in concentration while she made notes on a yellow legal pad, she hadn't heard him come in. He took the opportunity to drink in the sight.

The morning sun filtered through the window and illuminated her hair, turning the darker strands of blond to burnished gold. Her hand skimmed over the paper, making furious notes, and he recalled the feel of them moving over his skin. How they'd brought to life a need in him that he knew no other woman would be able to satisfy.

Just then, she turned toward him. Their gazes locked and held. Her warm, emerald eyes and the slight tilt of her lush red lips acted like a magnet on Jesse's senses. He found himself frozen in place, barely able to breathe. The need to feel her against him began to grow, until he had to clench his fists to keep from acting on it.

Outside a branch moved in a slight breeze and tapped the window behind Karen. She jumped and turned toward the noise, breaking the mesmerizing spell.

Jesse blinked, then filled his aching lungs with air. The fragrant odor of freshly brewed coffee drifted to him, and thankful for the distraction, he busied himself pouring a mugful. As nonchalantly as a man with hot sex on his mind could, he sat across from her and took a sip of the steaming brew to moisten his dry throat.

When he could safely speak again, he pointed at the yellow pages of notes in front of her. "What's all that?"

Having already decided that the faster they solved the mystery of Paul's death, the sooner she could leave and avoid more damage to her heart, Karen had been up most of the night working on Jesse's theory that Hank was involved.

"I thought if I made a list of everything we know so far, it would help us make some progress." She shuffled the papers and pointed at one that had *Hank* written across the top. "You may be right about Hank's involvement. Yesterday Elle told me she and Scott had gone to Hank's house to talk to him. Have you ever been there?"

Jesse shook his head and sipped from his coffee again.

Karen squirmed in her seat, trying to contain her excitement about what she had to tell him. "Elle said that Hank's house is much too elaborate for a man earning what he does. Also, Mrs. Thompson has some pretty impressive, not to mention expensive, clothes."

Jesse shrugged. "I'm not getting the connection to Paul."

"So . . . where does he get the money for all that?" She leaned forward and lowered her voice as if making sure she would not be overheard. "Elle's Air-Medi friend told her that small helicopters like the one that left the prints in the dirt up there are often used by drug runners. They're easy to get in and out of tight places quickly."

Jesse choked on his coffee. "Are you trying to tell me that Hank's running drugs out of the Preserve?"

Karen laid down her pencil and flashed him her best smug look. "Ex—actly."

Putting aside his coffee cup, he leaned on the table. His expression screamed skepticism. "That's pretty flimsy evidence, Karen. We can't go accusing him, no matter how angry we are, of something like that without more proof. And I don't think many juries would call a bad temper, an elaborate house, and wife with expensive tastes damning evidence."

Past the point of discussion and primed for action, Karen stood, gathered her papers, folded them and then stuffed them in the back pocket of her jeans. "Then I suggest we get a move on and find some evidence that is damning."

Jesse held up his hand. "And just where do you suggest we start?"

Karen slid back into the chair, her body tense with frustration at Jesse's lack of enthusiasm. "The ice caves."

"Why the ice caves?"

"Well, I've been thinking about where I'd hide drugs if I were Hank. I mean there aren't that many places up there. The ice caves are perfect. Protected, isolated, off the beaten path. And remember that pile of trash. Well, what if it's not trash?" She leaned back and crossed her arms.

He sighed and stood. "Well, one thing I can see is that you're not about to give up on this idea until we go look. Let's stop by Dave's first. We can borrow his ladder to climb down in there."

"Great idea! I'll call Elle and tell her where we're going."

Jesse laughed. "Are you sure you don't want to stop at the store for one of those big magnifying glasses, Dr. Watson?"

She glared at him and dialed the phone. After a brief conversation with her sister, she hung up. "Elle and Scott are going back to where we got shot at and look around. When we're done, I'll call her, and we can meet with them to compare notes."

Dave, dressed in his signature red and black plaid hunting shirt and worn jeans, looked across his kitchen table at them. "This is the craziest notion I ever heard. Hank mixed up with drug runners?" He shook his head. "Course, I suppose it would explain why he's so all fired determined to keep you away from the burn site. Wouldn't it?"

Karen flashed an I-told-you-so smile at Jesse, then turned to Dave. "That's exactly what I thought." She decided she might as well tell Dave everything Elle had told her during their brief phone conversation, some of which she hadn't even had a chance to tell Jesse yet. "Elle said the soil tested positive for pure gasoline. She figured it might have been used to start a backfire to control the burn."

Jesse shook his head. "No. Pure gasoline is never used for backfires. It's too volatile and too hard to control. Gasoline produces a suction effect that robs the fire of oxygen and results in a firestorm. A firefighter caught in the middle of the firestorm doesn't stand a chance of survival because of the extremely high temps. Rather than risking using the pure stuff, we mix three to four parts diesel fuel to one part gasoline and then spread it carefully with a drip torch." He paused for a moment. "Of course, if it were pure gasoline, it would account for the fact that Paul's fire shelter was never deployed. He didn't have time."

The idea of Paul trapped inside a raging, heat intense fire and not being able to find shelter made Karen want to cry. She'd long since realized that what she'd felt for Paul was not the same kind of love she felt for Jesse, but just the thought of him suffering through such an agonizing death made her heart ache for him.

"Karen? Are you okay?"

When she realized that Jesse had been talking to her, Karen started. "I'm fine. I was just thinking. What did you say?"

Jesse continued to stare at her, a questioning expression on his face. "Did Elle say anything else?"

Quickly, she pulled herself together. "Yes. Yes she did. She also checked Paul's autopsy report, and the cause of death was from a blow to the head, which the coroner thinks could have happened if a tree fell on him during the fire."

"Or if he'd been hit with a blunt object." Jesse muttered.

Frowning, he studied Karen. He was rapidly beginning to think Karen's theory might hold water.

Still looking like what Jesse interpreted as a bit dazed, Karen nodded her agreement.

Dave looked skeptical. "You two are doing a lot of speculating here. You got any proof besides the gas and the autopsy report? How would anyone get drugs up into the ice caves without me knowing it? I'd hear a helicopter landing up there."

Jesse was thoughtful for a moment. "You go into town on the

eleventh of every month to deposit your Social Security check, right?" It was common knowledge among the rangers that if you were out in the woods and were looking for a coffee break at Dave's, that the eleventh was not the time to drop by. Dave nodded. "Hank knows that. He could make sure the drugs came in that day."

"Maybe," Dave said, "but you still haven't connected him to the drugs. For that matter you don't know that there are any drugs in the cave."

Karen stood. "We will in a while. That is if you let us borrow your aluminum ladder." She turned to Dave. "Wanna come and see what we find?"

He laughed. "Nothing would please me more than to help you two solve this, but I've got chores that need seeing to. Besides, my old bones would never be able to take the cold down in those caves. When you bring back the ladder, you can fill me in."

"Deal," Karen said, kissed him on his ruddy, weathered cheek and then went through the cabin's door toward the tool shed.

Jesse followed her out, wondering if her overwhelming urgency to do this was motivated by a need to solve the mystery of Paul's death or the desire to get it over with so she could leave Bristol, and him. Her leaving was what he wanted, wasn't it? That should make him happy, shouldn't it?

But all it did was cover him with a veil of depression that made him want to double over in pain.

Chapter 13

Jesse had only gone a few yards up the road when he hit the steering wheel and mumbled a string of curses. Karen looked up from her notes and saw a car coming toward them. Thinking Jesse was upset at meeting another vehicle on the narrow road, she went back to her notes. Not until the car slowed, then stopped, and Jesse rolled down his window did she look up again.

Parked beside them was a pea green SUV. Just above Jesse's window, she could see the top of the insignia of the Adirondack Mountains Preserve. At the wheel was Hank Thompson, his stormy features announcing that he was not at all happy to see them.

"If you two are heading for the burn site, you might want to think twice about it. I've got two New York State Troopers posted up there with orders to arrest anyone trying to get on the site." His smile lacked warmth or humor.

Jesse returned the smile in kind. "We're just out for a ride."

Hank leaned back so her could see Karen. "A ride huh?" Then he looked at the roof of the car where they'd tied Dave's ladder. "With a ladder?"

"I borrowed the ladder from Dave to fix my TV antenna. Can't get crap on the tube, and cable hasn't made it out our way yet." Jesse mouthed the lie so easily that it made Karen uncomfortable. What else had he lied about?

"Well, just stay away from the burn site." Hank put the car in gear and moved past them down the mountain.

Karen turned around and watched him until he disappeared from sight around an outcropping of rocks on the side of the road. "Boy, you pulled that out of your hat. Unless I'm mistaken, you don't have a TV antenna."

"Nope. Em had satellite installed while she lived there, and when she moved out, she just transferred the account into my name." His Cheshire cat grin made her smile.

"Think Hank believed you?"

Jesse shrugged and put the car in gear. "We better not plan on it." He hit the gas, and the car lurched forward. "I'd rather not take the chance, so let's get this done as fast as we can. He may just decide to come back and check on us." He shifted gears. "If you're right about him, the less he thinks we know the better, and if he finds us down in the caves . . . ."

He glanced at Karen, and his blood ran cold. He was headed to a hole in the ground that was slick with ice, with a pregnant woman. As if that weren't bad enough, she planned to climb down in the hole with him. Had he completely lost what was left of his mind?

"When we get up there, I'll go down in the cave and check out that pile of trash, and you wait at the top for me."

Karen opened her mouth to protest, but he stopped her cold in her tracks.

"This is not open for discussion. You either do it my way, or I turn around, and we go home right now." He slowed the car to show her the seriousness of his threat.

She stared at him for a long moment, indecision written clearly on her face. He knew from the set of her jaw that she didn't like the idea of not being in the thick of things, but he was not about to back down. If anything happened to her or her baby . . . .

Well, it was something he didn't even want to think about, and if she stayed at the opening of the cave, then he wouldn't have to.

"Well? Is it a deal?"

She sighed and nodded with an abrupt dip of her head. "All right. But I don't have to like it."

Her bottom lip stuck out in a cute little pout that made him want to haul her into his arms and kiss her until she forgot about ice caves and hidden drugs and wildfires and anything else that filled her pretty head.

But he didn't. Jesse took a deep, steadying breath and dragged his gaze back to the road. For the rest of the drive up the mountain, he kept his mind on ice caves and off the woman sitting beside him. By the time they pulled into the parking lot, he had his body and his emotions under control again.

He stepped from the car, then reached in the backseat and grabbed one of the sweatshirts he'd thrown back there before they'd left the house. Karen grabbed the other one.

"You're not going to be needing that," he told her sternly.

"I know, but I might as well take it. Just in case."

For a time he just stared at Karen, unsure whether to believe her pledge to stay out of the caves or not.

Evidently, her impatience having gotten the best of her, she returned his glare. "I said I'd wait at the top, and I will. Are we going to sit here until Hank comes back and finds us or are we going to do what we came here for?"

Finally, satisfied that she would keep her word not to come down in the cave, he quickly slipped the sweatshirt on, then busied himself untying the ladder from the car's roof. Despite his admonishments not to, Karen insisted on helping him remove the ladder, and carry it and a flashlight into the woods. A steady stream of mist rising from the cave's opening marked its location.

Karen leaned over and peered down into the yawning opening. The cold air gushing up to meet her made her gasp. "The trash pile is still there."

Jesse looked over her shoulder. In the corner, tucked behind an outcropping of ice-covered rock was the cardboard they'd seen the last time they'd been here. A thin layer of ice had formed on it.

They both straightened at the same time, their faces inches apart. For a reason unknown to him, he forgot that he'd vowed to keep a safe distance between him and Karen. He grabbed her and sealed off her mouth with his. Her lips were warm, eager and clinging. They issued an unmistakable invitation that made him go weak in the knees. Though he would have liked nothing better than to follow where that kiss was begging him to go, he pulled away.

Though quick and fiery, the kiss reminded him of that afternoon in the woods. With that reminder came the echo of the shot that had nearly taken Karen from him forever. She would never be safe until they solved the mystery of Paul's death. That wasn't going to happen if Hank came back and found them.

Jesse gently put her away from him. "Help me drop the ladder into the cave."

Karen grabbed one side and together they lowered it into the opening, then wedged it between two rocks on the cave floor. Jesse put a foot on the top rung and tested it under his weight to make sure it wouldn't slide. Satisfied that it would stay put, he began a slow descent.

As Jesse descended lower and lower into the cave, the temperature took a drastic nosedive from the warm July air above to the intense cold necessary to sustain the frozen caves. He shivered and wished he'd brought something warmer than his sweatshirt. In that short period of time it took to climb down there, his finger joints had stiffened from grasping the cold metal of the ladder. When he reached the cave's floor, and while he rubbed his hands together to get his blood circulating and bring back the flexibility and warmth in his fingers, he took stock of his surroundings.

That he stood in a chamber frozen solid with ice and dripping with crystal icicles in the middle of July held a surreal quality, to say the least.

"You know," he said as he looked around him, "even though, when I was a kid, I spent hours exploring these caves. It's still blows me away."

"Reminisce later, Jesse." Karen's impatient voice echoed around the cave. "What do you see?"

"Nothing yet."

With the circulation restored in his hands, he turned toward the cardboard. The haphazardly piled pieces of cardboard, some soda cans, and an empty Twinkies box had no doubt been discarded by some picnickers or campers and resembled nothing more than what it was at first glance, discarded trash. Cautiously, he moved the torn cardboard aside with the toe of his boot. Beneath it was a large black plastic bag. More garbage?

"Is that what I think it is?" Karen asked from above. Evidently his body temperature had heated the air and dissipated some of the mist so she could see better.

"I don't know. It could just be more trash."

"Open it," she urged, her voice elevated with excitement.

Kneeling on the cardboard, Jesse, his own excitement rising right along with hers, undid the wire tie at the top of the bag and spread it open. Inside where what looked like blocks of chalk wrapped in clear plastic. His heart rate tripled. He'd suspected Karen might be right, but until now, he'd been skeptical.

"Looks like someone's drug stash all right." He picked one up and turned to show her.

He ran into a solid wall of woman. Karen had climbed down and was standing right behind him. For a moment, his breath caught, but he quickly shook off the instant sexual reaction. "I thought I told you to wait up there?" He motioned angrily toward the ladder.

"I had to come down here and see it up close for myself." She glanced at the brick he held, then grinned, and kissed him full on the mouth. "We did it!"

His senses spun. Jesse shook his head as much to clear away the effects of her kiss as to stop her from believing this meant anything more than it did. "Did what? We found a drug stash. That's it. There's no connection between this and Paul's death or this and Hank's part in any of it."

She drew away. "What about the copter prints? They're proof that someone landed at the burn site, someone who didn't belong there. Elle said her friend told her that was the size helicopter sometimes used to transport drugs."

Jesse sighed. He wanted more than anything to tell her they could leave here and have Hank arrested. But he couldn't.

"*Sometimes* is the operative word. We have no proof that the chopper landed there for that purpose or any other. There could be any number of explanations for those tracks being there." Her smile melted. He dropped the brick back into the trash bag, then took her shoulders in his hands. "Karen, listen to me. We can't jump to any conclusions. Finding these drugs doesn't mean Hank put them here or that Hank killed Paul. The burn site is miles from here. I'm afraid the only substantial connection between the two right now is a rutted logging road through the woods."

Karen looked deflated. Jesse could have cut his tongue out for being the cause, but, despite how it looked to their untrained eyes, he couldn't let her believe they were any closer to Paul's killer than before they climbed down here.

Suddenly she brightened. "Fingerprints. Hank's fingerprints must be on the drugs. He put them down here after the chopper dropped them off." Jesse frowned. "Okay, *maybe* he put them down here. Even if he didn't, whoever did would have left their prints behind."

He'd concede that point to her. "Okay, let's take one of the bricks to Elle and have her get it dusted for prints. That way, instead of playing this guessing game, we'll at least have a definite person to look at." He leaned over to pick up the discarded brick.

A noise from behind them stopped him. Swinging toward the sound, he saw the ladder disappearing up the steep wall of the cave.

"What the—Hey, put that back." He lunged for the ladder, but missed. When Karen appeared at his side, he shoved her, pinning her against the wall with his body. "Stay back," he hissed under his breath, his gaze locked on the opening above them. "Who's there?" he called.

As Jesse listened, his blood ran cold and not from the temperature of the cave. No one responded. No sound came from overhead. No voice. No footsteps. It was as if a ghost had appeared and pulled the ladder up.

"Are they gone?" Karen's quivering whisper brushed the back

of his neck.

He could feel her body trembling against him. Whether it was with cold or fear, he didn't know. "I think so." Did he dare stick his head out and possibly end up on the wrong end of a bullet? Did he have a choice? They certainly couldn't remain here, cowering in the cold. "I'm going to try to climb up and see if anyone's still there."

"No!" Her fingers clutched his arm, digging painfully into the flesh beneath the material of his sweatshirt.

"I have to. We can't just stay here." Her hand tightened its hold. "Karen, let go. Now!"

She shivered, and her hand loosened its hold. "Please be careful."

Jesse edged out from beneath the overhang under which they'd taken cover, then, with his belly plastered tightly against the cold stone, slid along the wall, his gaze fixed on the opening above. Despite the cold, beads of nervous perspiration broke out on his forehead.

Just below the opening, Jesse worked the toe of his boot into an indentation in the rocks. Finding handholds, he slowly pulled himself up the wall, trading handholds for footholds. The going was slow and tedious. He'd only gone a few feet when his fingertips went numb from the icy rocks. As the cold seeped into him, he could feel his grip became more and more difficult to sustain.

He'd nearly reached the top when his fingers slipped. Helpless to stop himself, he tumbled back to the cave's floor. He landed hard on his behind, with his foot twisted under him. Pain radiated from his ankle.

Karen cried out. Immediately she hurried to him, knelt at his side, and supported him while he struggled to sit up. "Are you okay?"

Ribbing his stinging posterior, he said, "I think so." He tried to stand. As if someone had shoved a hot poker in his ankle, sharp pain shot up his leg. Unable to stop himself, he crumpled back to the floor. Grimacing and smiling weakly up at her, he said, "Guess I was wrong."

"What is it?"

"I twisted my ankle. I think it's sprained. Let me lean on you." She wrapped her arm around his waist, and he put his arm around her shoulders. Only then did he realize she had neglected to put on her sweatshirt and was shivering uncontrollably. "You're cold." He sat down, then slipped his sweatshirt over his head and handed it to her. "Here, put this on."

She looked at his cotton shirt and then shook her head. "No, you need it. You're the one who's hurt."

"Karen, hurt doesn't mean I can't stand the cold. I work outside all year round. I'm used to it. Besides, I'm not pregnant." He shoved the shirt at her. "No arguments. Put it on."

Karen took the shirt and slid it over her head. "Who do you think took the ladder?"

Shaking his head, Jesse held his silence. He could speculate, but that wasn't going to prove anything. Right now, they needed to find a way out.

"We'll worry about that after we get out of here," he told her as calmly as he could.

Looking around her, Karen's initial fear grew into a tight knot in her chest. "How? I think you've already proven that we can't climb those walls. They're too steep. Besides you'd never make it with that injured ankle."

Jesse glanced around, his complexion pale with the pain. "Then we'll have to look for another way."

"Great idea, but you can't walk."

A pain-filled groan escaped from Jesse as he pulled himself to his feet with her help and that of the wall behind him. "I don't have a choice. It's going to be dark soon, and we can't stay here all night. We'll freeze to death, which is what I'm sure whoever took the ladder had in mind."

"Wait." Karen slid her hands up the sleeves of the sweatshirt.

The resulting image, as she twisted and turned inside the shirt, was like two pigs fighting in a gunnysack. Despite their situation, Jesse stared in rapt amusement. After several minutes of indescribable gyrations, she pulled her hand from beneath the sweatshirt.

"Hold this," she said and handed him her blouse. The hand disappeared under the sweatshirt again.

He took the blouse, and watched while she replaced her arms in the sleeves of the sweatshirt. "What?" she said, when she caught his amused expression.

"Nothing. That's just got to be the most amazing thing I've ever seen."

She took back her blouse and began ripping it into long strips. "Then you can't have led a very exciting life, Kingston."

Until he'd met her, his life had been anything but exciting. Since Karen had come into it, it seemed nothing was even close to ordinary. Every breath he took was a new and exciting adventure. Every day special, something to look forward to. Every sunrise brighter and all because he knew she'd be there to share it. When she left, there would be a huge hole in his life that he might never fill again.

But he couldn't tell her any of that. Because then she'd stay and then he'd end up hurting her or alienating her like his father had done to him, or even worse, whoever was trying to kill them might be successful.

But it doesn't have to be like that, Emily's voice reminded him. *You are not like him.*

"Jesse?" He started and looked at Karen. "Sit down."

He lowered himself to the cave floor. Karen removed his boot and sock, then took the strips she'd ripped and began binding his ankle. "This will help reduce the pain and support your ankle so you can walk. When I've finished, put your boot back on, but don't tie it too tight. It's probably going to swell, so if it feels too tight, take the boot off. Hopefully you can keep it on long enough to get us out of here."

If I can find the way out, he thought, watching her wind the material round and round his ankle. But he didn't tell Karen that. No sense smashing her hope until he had to, but, since the last time he'd been here was when he was about fourteen, his expectations of finding a way out were pretty low.

She tied off the last strip, then handed him his sock and boot. He slipped them both on, remembering to tie the boot loosely.

"Okay. Try standing on it." Karen looped her arm under his and helped hoist him to his feet.

Tentatively, he put his weight on it. It hurt, but not nearly as bad as it had without the bindings. Certainly, the pain was tolerable enough for them to explore the cave for another exit.

"Let's see where this goes," he said, pointing at the passageway that lead off to their right.

"I thought you said you knew these caves from when you were a kid."

"A kid, Karen. I haven't been down here for years. Right now, I'm going on instinct." He took a limping step toward her and grimaced as pain shot up his leg.

"Lean on me, and it'll help keep the weight off your foot." Without waiting for him to comply, Karen wrapped her arm around his waist.

Jesse looped his arm around her shoulders. Her hair brushed his cheek, and the smell of her shampoo drifted up to him. He swayed. This togetherness was probably not the best idea. He removed his arm from her shoulder and limped a few feet away.

"Let me try this alone. With all this ice underfoot, we could both end up going down and I don't want you hurt, too."

Without looking at her, he hobbled off toward the end of the cave that seemed to continue on. Karen followed silently. They'd walked for some time, twisting and turning through the frozen cave, ducking under icy stalactites that hung from the ceiling like long crystal fingers, stepping over slick rocks, and making decisions about which branch of the tunnel to follow.

Jesse knew the caves ran under the ground and every now and again broke through the surface, but when they came to such a spot where the ground opened and the sky was visible, the walls were still too steep to climb out.

They pushed on. But the farther they went, the darker it became outside. Without the meager warmth from up above, the more the temperature dropped.

Jesse looked over his shoulder to check on Karen. She was keeping pace with his slow progress with no trouble, but her body was shaking so bad, it looked as if she might fall apart. As soon as she saw him looking at her, she stiffened and glared back as if daring him to point out that she was cold. He thought he knew how he could get her to allow him to warm her up.

Jesse turned to continue their trek, then intentionally stumbled and leaned against a rock. Karen hurried to him. Her shaking hand on his arm felt like an ice cube. If he didn't get her out of here soon, she'd have pneumonia.

"Are you okay?" her voice held such concern that for a second, he felt guilty about his deception.

He forced a good imitation of a weak smile. "My ankle is throbbing like a toothache." Truth be known, it did hurt like hell, but the pain was nothing he couldn't stand.

"Then let's rest."

"No, we can't. It's getting darker and colder by the minute. We have to get out of here."

A heartbeat later she said, "Then put your arm around my shoulder."

Jesse did as she instructed and was surprised by the cold he could feel coming off her body. He gave her a hug that nestled her firmly against him.

She smiled up at him. "This is a hell of a time to make a pass, Kingston."

"Was I that obvious?" They both laughed and the tension that and been between them all day vanished. "I'm freezing my buns off. Let's get the hell out of here," he said and pulled her with him down the cave tunnel.

A while later they stopped to rest Jesse's ankle. It felt as if they'd been walking for hours. The last surface opening they passed under had still spilled sunlight into the cave, but each time they passed under one of those surface holes, the sunlight had become weaker and the shadows longer.

To keep her waning hope of them ever finding a way out and her guilt for having gotten them into this mess to begin with at bay, Karen asked the question that had been burning in the back of her mind since she saw the ladder disappear over the rim of the cave. The question Jesse had made it quite obvious he hadn't wanted to answer the last time she'd asked it.

"Do you think Hank took the ladder?" She didn't look at Jesse, but instead concentrated on tucking her hands in her armpits to get them warm.

There was a momentary pause, then Jesse sighed. "Isn't it obvious? Hank decided he couldn't take our word for what we were doing and decided to follow us. When he saw what we'd discovered, he decided to let us freeze to death down here and save his neck. Hell, no one would find us for weeks, maybe months, and when they did, we'd just look like a couple of popsicles." He glanced at her. "Wouldn't be the first time it happened."

Karen shivered and not from the cold. How could anyone be so heartless? But she was slowly leaning that some people would do anything to cover their criminal tracks—even murder. Fear twisted in a knot in her stomach, but she couldn't let Jesse see it.

Instead of allowing the fear to show, she avoided his gaze. "But we don't have any proof it was him." She sighed. "We're right back where we were before we came down here."

"Looks that way." Jesse sighed and leaned back against the icy wall.

A draft of warm air caressed her cheeks. Karen looked up, gasped, and pointed over Jesse's shoulder.

Chapter 14

The opening was about five feet from the floor of the cave. Though a simple climb for Karen, it proved to be more difficult for Jesse with his injured ankle. With Karen's help, they got him to the top and back into the balmy warmth of an early summer evening.

For a while, they sat there, catching their breath and enjoying the return of sensation to their chilled bodies. Finally, Jesse pulled himself to his feet. He needed to get Karen away before whoever trapped them returned to see if they were still alive, and maybe finished the job.

"Let's get out of here," he said, reaching for her hand and pulling her up beside him. He stalled their departure. "Karen?"

"Yes?"

"Thanks."

She looked at him her confusion evident in her expression. "For what?"

He almost said for everything. *For being who you are. For understanding who I am and not forcing me to talk about it.* Habits die hard. Instead of saying what was in his heart he settled on, "Just—thank you."

After studying him for a moment, she gave a brief nod, put her arm around Jesse's waist to support him and said, "Let's go."

Together, they hobbled through the thick growth of wild blueberries, mountain laurel bushes, and scrub pine. A rosy glow covered the western sky and the shadowed fingers of twilight were growing longer. Evening was quickly approaching. From past experience in these mountains, he knew the darkness would come fast and when it did, it would be absolute.

Jesse hurried the pace. In very few minutes, they wouldn't be able to see their hands in front of their faces, and he had no desire to be in such a vulnerable position. Rather than question him, Karen seemed to sense his urgency and kept pace.

Finally, they stepped out into the parking lot. He breathed a sigh of relief when he saw the car right where they'd left it. But when he recalled the last time they'd been here and the incident with the brakes, the knot in his stomach returned.

"I'll drive," Karen announced, holding her hand out for the keys.

For a fraction of a second, he wanted to refuse, but with his right ankle injured, he'd never be able to operate the brakes going down the mountain. Without argument, he gave them to her, but with a condition.

"Let me check the brake lines before we leave, just in case."

Karen nodded and climbed into the driver's seat. She watched him disappear below the front end of the car. He emerged a few seconds later and nodded at her. He repeated the same process in the rear, then came to her side window.

"Hand me the flashlight in the glove box and hit the hood release." Pointing a finger at the lever's location, he took the flashlight she'd handed him and waited until he heard the hood pop open. Before he limped to the front of the car, he leaned down. "Put the window up and lock your door."

The apprehension lacing his voice seeped into her frazzled nerves. Without argument, she did as he'd instructed. At the front of the car, he lifting the hood, secured it with the rod support, then disappeared beneath it.

Insidious, clammy fingers of fear crawled over Karen's skin. She shivered and stared into the inky night, methodically searching the deepening darkness for signs of life—human life. When she was reasonably satisfied that they were alone, she slid down in the seat. Through the slit between the back of the raised hood and the windshield, Karen watched as Jesse tugged on wires, tested hoses, and did a visual search of the engine. Then he closed the hood and got in the passenger seat.

"Everything looks okay. Let's go home."

The way he said *home* sent a gush of warmth through Karen and dispelled the fear instantly. *Home.* As if they were an old married couple out for an evening. Now, the evening was over and they were going *home—together*.

But it wasn't *their* home. It was Jesse's home. Her home was in New York City. She had to remember that or she'd end up with a broken heart for sure. Then again, her heart had already been split in half. How much more could it ache?

The chill returned.

She started the car and headed down the mountain.

At the house, Karen took a shower and then went straight to bed. She felt guilty for not sticking around to help dress Jesse's ankle, but she couldn't stand the thought of being near him and touching him, not when she felt as if her world had started to crumble around her.

She lay awake for hours with her mind racing between wanting to catch whoever had killed Paul and trapped them in the cave and knowing that when they did, her time here would be over. She'd have to return to New York—without Jesse.

Tears ran down her cheeks and soaked her pillow. Why couldn't life be simple? Why did it always have to be a test of how well human strength could stand up to adversity?

Jesse opened a beer and flopped on the sofa. His ankle throbbed in time to his heartbeat. He suspected the bandage Karen had put on was too tight, but he had neither the strength nor the desire to fix it. He ignored the pain and gulped down another long swallow of the icy beer.

Karen. God, she hovered on the edge of his mind like a half-formed dream. But she wasn't a dream. She was flesh and blood real. And, as much as he hated to admit it, she was part of him. The best part.

Maybe if he got roaring, out-of-his-mind drunk he could

forget the color of her eyes, the feel of her skin, the sound of her laughter, the way her hair shone like gold in the sunlight. Maybe if he numbed his senses with alcohol, he'd find some peace of mind. Maybe then he could erase the images of them wrapped in each other's arms in the age old ritual of love.

He knew better. Karen would remain in his head, and only if he concentrated on something else would he find a modicum of peace.

With concentrated determination, he thought about the ice caves, and who could have taken the ladder, leaving them to freeze to death. Hank had seen the ladder on top of the car, seen the direction they were headed. Had he seen through Jesse's flimsy explanation about the TV antenna, put two and two together, and figured out that they were going to look in the caves? Had Hank been planning to wait until he was sure they were dead from hypothermia, then come back and get his drug stash?

Jesse started to take a drink and stopped, the bottle halfway to his mouth. If Hank was hustling drugs out of the woods by the burn site, how was it no one had caught him? The area wasn't that isolated, especially with the fire towers and the patrols. This time of year was especially prime for forest fires, so the patrols were more frequent. Then again, who would know the schedule of the patrols better than Hank?

He could have made sure the drops were done during times when they wouldn't be detected. Someone should have seen suspicious activity up there. Maybe Paul saw him and that's why Hank killed him. Could that be why Paul walked into a fire he knew had a chance of killing him? He knew Hank was due to have a drug shipment come in, and Paul was trying to catch him in the act?

Jesse checked the time. Twelve-twenty-two. Too late to pay Hank a house call tonight, but after he took Dave's ladder back in the morning, he'd go see his old boss and wring the truth out of him.

The next morning, Karen wandered into the kitchen in her robe and slippers. Jesse was showered and dressed and sitting at the table reading the newspaper. His still damp hair glistened in the morning sun pouring through the window behind him, and she could smell the fragrance of his pine-scented soap all the way across the room.

Her breath lodged in her throat, as if her ability to breathe had been stolen from her. With effort, she shook loose the urge to go to him. Instead, she took a deep breath, and pulled a mug from the cabinet and then poured a cup of hot, black, invigorating coffee. Normally, Jesse's strong coffee was like drinking tar, but today, she needed the extra jolt of caffeine to keep her mind on things that didn't make her feel like someone was tearing her heart out.

She took a seat across from him. "How's your ankle?" The sip of the coffee she took scalded her tongue. Setting the cup aside to cool, she folded her hands on the table and waited for him to reply.

"Tender." He finished reading whatever article had caught his eye, folded the paper, and laid it next to his placemat. "How are you feeling after our adventure yesterday?"

"Fine." Small talk. Good grief, this was pathetic. They couldn't even carry on a conversation anymore. Next thing she knew they'd be discussing the weather. "So, what's happening today?"

Jesse sipped his coffee, then took a bite of his toast and chewed thoughtfully. He swallowed, but made no attempt to answer her. She waited.

Finally, he spoke. "I'm going to find Hank and talk to him."

"What exactly do you expect him to tell you?"

"I don't know. I just know I need to talk to him."

"I'll get dressed then."

She started to get up, but he caught her arm and pushed her gently back into her chair. "No. You're staying here."

Rebellion erupted in her like a volcano gathering the power to blow wide open. She wanted to hear what Hank would say, see if he tripped himself up, see if he said anything that they could use to connect him to the recent incidents and Paul's death.

"Now, wait just a minute." The glare she sent his way underlined her anger.

Jesse stopped her protest cold. "This is not a point of discussion. I need you here." *Out of harm's way*, he added to himself.

"For what?" She fairly spat the words at him.

Jesse cringed. He knew how much she wanted to be in on this face-off with Hank. He hadn't expected her to take this isolation from the center of things lightly, but he had to convince her not to go.

"I need you to call Elle and see if they found anything in the woods where we were shot at. Anything the police missed." He watched as bit of the rebellion in her face eased.

"Can't you wait while I call, then let me go with you?"

He stood and shook his head. "I'm going up to retrieve Dave's ladder before I go to talk to Hank. Both times we've gone near those ice caves together something has happened. I'm not taking any chances this time."

She stood and faced him nose-to-nose, anger shooting from her eyes. "So you're going alone. What if something else happens? I'll never know because you just want me to sit here like a good little girl."

"Don't insult me or yourself." He took her shoulders. "I don't want you to be a good little girl. I want you safe." He stared into her gorgeous green eyes and tried not to think of life without her, inevitable as it eventually would become when all reason for her to stay ceased to exist. Suddenly the pain of thinking about her ultimate return to the city became more than he could bear, and he hauled her to him. "I just want you safe," he whispered into her hair.

The stiffness drained from her like someone had pulled the plug on her anger. She melted against him and then snaked her arms around his waist. As though sensing his pain, she held him close.

"I'll be here when you get back," she mumbled against his chest. "I promise." Then she tightened her grip. "Just promise me you'll be careful." She leaned away and looked up at him with pleading eyes.

He kissed the tip of her nose and grinned. "I'll be careful. You just stay here so I don't have to worry about you and can concentrate on what I have to do."

He picked up his car keys and strode out the door.

Karen watched him leave. Tears welled up in her eyes, but she blinked them away. As her gaze followed his car out of the driveway and down the road, she fought off the feeling of dread that suddenly settled in the pit of her stomach and whispered, "I love you Jesse Kingston. And you damned well better come back."

Two fear-filled hours later, as if heeding her repeated command, Jesse drove back into the driveway. Those had to have been the most stressful hours Karen had ever spent. One minute she'd been sure he was okay, the next, equally certain something terrible had happened to him. Unable to bear the thought of losing someone else she loved, she'd teetered on the edge of breaking down totally. It surprised her that she hadn't worn a path in the floor while pacing off the long parade of minutes.

But that was over. Jesse was home. Disregarding the look of relief that must have shown on her face, Karen took a deep breath, then raced to the back porch to meet him. She stopped short at the top of the steps, resisting the urge to throw herself into his arms, to feel the substance of him aligned with her own body, tangible assurance that he actually had come back in one piece.

As Jesse closed the car door behind him, then glanced at her, she noted the discouraged twist to his mouth. "What did Hank say?' she asked as he climbed the porch steps.

A mocking laugh burst from him. "Nothing."

"What do you mean nothing?"

"I mean I picked up the ladder and took it to Dave, who wasn't home. So, I left and drove to the ranger station. Hank wasn't there, nor was he at home. In short, I couldn't talk to Hank because I couldn't find him." He spat the explanation at her and raked his fingers through his hair in a frustrated gesture. "Did you call Elle?"

Karen shook her head. "Yes, but with no better results than you got." The look of defeat that came over him made her wish she had better news. "Elle wasn't there. Neither was Scott. Considering the time I called, I'm assuming they were out for breakfast. I'll try again in a bit."

"Great," he mumbled and threw open the back door and stomped into the house.

She followed him back inside. "Jesse, you can talk to Hank another time. There's no rush."

He stopped so quickly, she almost ran into him. "No rush? I thought you were the one who said you wanted to get answers so we could get this settled."

"Well, I was. I am. But I also know that we can't have all the answers at the exact moment we want them. We have to be a bit patient."

"I'm all out of patience, Karen." The look on his face was so fierce that Karen made a gesture to step back, but he wasn't about to allow her to move away. Instead, he snatched her by the shoulders and pulled her close to his face. "Don't you get it? I want you out of here," he ground out between clenched teeth. He set her from him and walked away.

Karen felt as though she'd just taken a body blow. Pain, sharp and agonizing, shot through her. She'd strongly sensed from his actions since that day in the woods that he'd regretted making love with her, but until this moment, she hadn't been able to substantiate her suspicions, nor gauge just how much he regretted it.

Chapter 15

Jesse sat on the edge of his bed. He knew he'd hurt Karen with his blunt announcement, but his frustration with not finding Hank had been ruling his tongue and not his head. Taking it out on her had been inexcusable, but at the same time he had to admit what he'd said was true.

He did want her out of here as soon as possible, before the jerk who'd been trying to stop them for finding out about Paul was successful in one of his attempts on their lives. Sending her away would be like tearing out a piece of his soul, but letting her stay and losing her forever would be worse. So what if she hated him? At least she'd be alive.

However, he could have been gentler about the way he'd told her, and he needed to apologize. Jesse stood, sighed, and went into the living room.

Karen was curled in the corner of the couch. He'd expected tears, but her cheeks were dry and her stare blank. She made no move to acknowledge that he'd come into the room. He sat down in the chair opposite the couch, placed his forearms on his thighs and searched for the words to explain.

"Karen, I—We need to talk about—" The shrill ringing of the phone cut him off. "Damn!" He reached for the receiver. Out of the corner of his eye, he saw Karen raise her head and turn toward him. "Hello."

Karen watched his expressions closely as he talked with the caller. After a few moments of muffled conversation, he hung up and stood.

"That was Dave. He says he convinced Hank to talk with me. They're waiting for me in the ice caves parking lot." Torn between staying and making things right with Karen and going to see what Hank had to say, he took a few hesitant steps toward the door. "I still want to talk to you when I get back."

She said nothing, simply nodded, then averted her gaze. That she never even asked to come with him spoke volumes. He'd really hurt her and in doing so, perhaps alienated her to a point far beyond anything he could ever repair.

As Jesse drove to the ice caves, he played over in his mind what Hank could possibly want to tell him. That the drugs were his? That he'd killed Paul to keep him quiet? If so, what could Dave possibly have said to him that would have changed Hank's mind and made him want to talk to Jesse? It just didn't make any sense.

Jesse finally decided that he was selling himself a bill of goods. Hank wouldn't confess. He probably just wanted to warn Jesse off again and had enlisted Dave's help to convince him. Jesse could easily see this becoming another screaming match between him and his ex-boss. Still having vivid memories of how much their last confrontation had upset Karen, he was glad she hadn't asked to come with him.

He closed his mind to thoughts of Karen, unable to think of her without experiencing a knife-sharp pain slice through him at the thought of losing the only person he had ever loved unconditionally. Instead, he looked off into the forests.

The familiar smell of pine filled the car. Always before, that smell had brought a peace to his soul that nothing else could. Today it reminded him that the sound of Karen's laughter brought him that same peace. The sunlight warming him as it poured through the windshield couldn't hold a candle to the warmth of Karen's smile. Even the bird's song dimmed in comparison to her voice whispering in his ear as they made love.

When had she replaced all the things that had filled this forest that he'd called home for so long?

But had it been his home or had it just been another hideout he'd used to avoid life? He recalled telling Karen that Mother Nature was safe. She didn't judge, and she didn't expect more than he could give. Although it was true, Mother Nature couldn't give him kids or be there for him when life closed in or share his old age. Karen could. But could he take that chance and put his heart on the line again?

What had Emily told him?

You're never going to be able to let that love out until you conquer your apprehension about being hurt. Not until you force your way through that can you get to the rest of your life. You have to bite the bullet and love freely, unconditionally and without fear, and hope you won't be hurt because life doesn't come with guarantees, Jesse. It only comes with a reasonable expectation of happiness and the human ability to find it. Believe me, it's well worth the risks.

Had he found that happiness with Karen? Was he about to throw it all away because of an old hurt that should have been buried with Frank Kingston, but that Jesse had kept alive by reliving his childhood memories and comparing everyone to his father? His father was dead and so should be the pain he'd caused Jesse. His sisters cared, but he'd been pushing them away. And now, he was pushing Karen away.

Yes, he was an unhappy man, but he was unhappy because of his own fears, fears he'd kept vivid in his mind long past the time when they should have been put to rest, and as a result of that fear, he'd isolated himself from human emotion. Was he willing to take the risks that Emily had so fervently proclaimed worth it? The admission came hard, but he knew that the happiness that had always eluded him would never be his unless he took a chance on love.

He needed to look life in the eye and take whatever it had to offer. He loved Karen, and he'd be damned if he'd lose her because of something a bitter old man did too many years ago to matter anymore. Suddenly, he felt as if the weight of the world had been lifted from his shoulders.

A smile creased his face. When he got back, he and Karen would have a talk all right. He still wanted her to leave for her own safety, but as soon as this was settled, he'd go after her.

When Jesse pulled into the parking lot, he spotted Dave's black and red plaid shirt even before he stepped fully out of the bushes.

Dave approached the car and then leaned down to peer inside. "Karen didn't come with you?"

Jesse climbed from the car and shook his head. "No, I didn't what her here." He looked around. "Where's Hank?"

Dave pointed over his shoulder in the direction of the caves. "Back there waiting for you." When Jesse made a move to start through the scrub pine, Dave stopped him. "Don't expect too much from him. He's not in much of a position to tell you anything."

Jesse frowned. "What the hell does that mean? Did you drag me up here for nothing? I came here expecting answers about Paul's death."

Dave smiled. "Oh, you'll get answers, my boy. Maybe not the ones you were expecting or want to hear, but you'll get your answers."

"Well then, let's go. Some answers are better than nothing." Anxious to get this over with so he could get back to settle things with Karen, Jesse pushed past Dave and headed for the caves.

They'd gone a few yards into the scrub and just started down a small dip in the terrain that led to the caves, when Jesse spied what looked like a shoe protruding from under one of the bushes.

"What the hell . . . ?" He stepped around the bushes and saw Hank's body crumpled on the ground. Blood seeped from a wound on his head. It looked as though he'd been hit by something.

Jesse leaned down to examine the head wound closer. It was deep and had been bleeding profusely, but now, the blood seeped slowly from the gaping wound. That could only mean one thing. When Jesse put his fingers to Hank's throat, he couldn't find a heartbeat.

137

Not ready to give Hank up for dead, even though in his heart he knew it was too late, Jesse scooped his boss' limp body up in his arms and turned to Dave. "We need to get him to a—"

A grim-faced Dave faced Jesse with a gun pointed at his heart. "I'm afraid that's not going to be possible, my boy."

Karen had made up her mind right after Jesse left that when he came back, she'd be gone. Staying here and feeling her heart shatter a little at a time was not something she wanted to do. There was nothing left to talk about. Nothing. Jesse obviously didn't want her. He'd made that very clear. And if he didn't want her, she certainly wasn't going to stay. All that would get her was more heartache.

Besides, she had a baby to worry about and lately, it had taken second place to Jesse. She'd move to the motel with Elle and Scott and wait to find out what Hank had told Jesse about Paul's death. Then she'd hit the road home.

As far as finding out about Paul's family, she'd just have to find some other way. She wasn't sure what that way would be, but she knew who it wouldn't be: Jesse Kingston. Even if she never found Paul's family, she'd finally put things into perspective. She had Elle and Scott, and her father, and that should be more than enough family for any baby.

Throwing her suitcase on the bed, she began removing her clothes from the dresser when there was a knock on the door. Jesse? For a moment her heart sped up. That tiny flame of hope that hadn't quite burned out, flickered. But then common sense set in. Jesse had no reason to knock on his own door.

Before she ever reached the door, she could see Elle peering in through the glass panel. Karen swung the door open. "Elle, what are you doing here?"

Elle skirted her and barged into the house. "Where's Jesse?"

Karen closed the door. "He's not here. Dave called him. Hank wanted to talk to him. Why?"

"I wanted to show him this to see if he recognized it."

Rummaging in her pocket, Elle pulled something out and held it out to Karen. "Scott and I checked the woods up where you were shot at. I don't know how the cops missed it, but my bloodhound of a husband found this hooked on a thorn bush about four hundred yards from where you were that day."

Karen looked down at Elle's outstretched palm, which held a ragged piece of red and black plaid flannel cloth no bigger than a dime.

"Scott said that because it's not faded from the sun or rain, he doubts it was there long. He figured it was torn from something the shooter was wearing."

As Karen listened to Elle's explanation, something tugged at her mind, but remained tantalizingly just beyond her grasp.

"Do you recognize it?" Elle asked.

Karen frowned. "I don't know."

She took the cloth from Elle, fingered it for a second, then sat down at the kitchen table. As Karen studied it, she racked her brain for that detail that lingered just beyond her reach. This color shirt was very common in this haven for hunters. Everyone wore them so they could be spotted easily in the woods and wouldn't be mistaken for an animal.

She'd been about to give up when an image of Dave standing in his driveway flashed in front of here. Jesse had said Dave always wore that type of shirt. The rangers even called it the *Dave-shirt* because they'd never seen him in anything else.

But Dave was nice man, gentle and kind. He'd never shoot at them. Would he? Karen pressed her fingers against her suddenly throbbing temples.

Her sister's hand came to rest on her shoulder. "Karen? What is it? Do you know who that could belong to?" Elle's questions penetrated the fog that had gathered around Karen's mind.

Karen raised her gaze to meet her sister's. "I'm not sure."

She didn't what to believe that Dave had anything to do with any of what had been happening to them in the last few days. Then little things began seeping into her mind, little things that couldn't be explained away.

Dave had warned Jesse off right after the brakes had been cut. Dave had scoffed at the idea that the trash she and Jesse had seen in the ice caves could be drugs. Dave had known they were going to the caves to investigate the trash.

Then something else started to formulate in her mind, something she and Jesse should have seen long ago. Dave said he never heard a chopper the day of the fire, but because of the fire's location, it must have flown right over his cabin. If, as he'd said they always did, shook his windows, he couldn't have missed it. Unless he didn't. Unless he knew it was coming and why.

Her blood froze in her veins. "Oh, my God!"

"What?" Elle clutched her arm. "What is it, Karen?"

"Dave. The shirt is Dave's. Jesse just went to meet him." She vaulted to her feet and then headed for the door.

"Karen, where are you going? Karen?" Elle followed her to the door. "Dammit, Karen, answer me."

"To warn Jesse. Call the police, Elle, and have them meet us in the ice caves parking lot."

Chapter 16

"Put him down, Jesse." Dave used the barrel of the gun to motion to Jesse where he wanted him to put Hank's limp body. "It's just a bump on the head. He'll come around in a bit."

Despite the stark fear lapping at his insides, Jesse glared at Dave. He had no idea that the blow to Hank's head had not just knocked him out. "He's not going to come around, Dave. You killed him. He's dead."

"Since you're not a doctor . . . ." Dave reached in the pocket of his bib overalls and pulled out a length of rope, then tossed it to Jesse. "Tie him up. Just in case you're wrong, I don't want him coming to and trying to be a hero like Paul did. And make sure it's tight. If he gets loose, I will kill him, and I'm sure you don't want that."

Jesse caught the rope. "You gonna kill me, too? Is that the plan? Make sure you don't leave anyone alive to tell the authorities that you killed Hank and Paul?" Anger motivated his words, anger at this man who had pretended to be his friend, to be Paul's and Hank's friend, and who Jesse was now sure had killed both of them. "Is that why you killed Paul? He was on to your drug business?"

An almost maniacal grin twisted Dave's mouth. This was not the Dave that Jesse knew. "Guilty, I'm afraid. Your friend got too nosey. Just like Hank, and you, and that sweet Karen. I tried to warn you off, but you wouldn't listen. Then I tried to scare you away, and you didn't take that to heart either." He shook his head. "Too bad she didn't come with you. Now I'll have to waste more time finding her and making sure she doesn't talk."

Fury erupted inside Jesse like a smoldering volcano. Realizing that infuriating Dave with curses and spewing his anger at the man would do him no good, Jesse tamped it down.

Still, his barely controlled rage smoldered inside. The bastard had been posing as their friend, while all the time he'd been taking potshots at them, trashing Karen's room, cutting their brake lines, and trapping them in a freezing cave. And now he was going to kill Karen?

Jesse shook his head to clear away the red haze of rage. "Why? Why did you do all this?"

"A man gets tired of living hand to mouth on the measly check that the government sends him once a month. If it hadn't been for hunting, I'd have been eating cat food out of tin cans to survive. That's no way for a decent man to live. No way for any man to live." He motioned at the rope Jesse still held. "Tie him up."

"No." Let him shoot. He refused to further dishonor Hank's corpse by trussing him up like a Thanksgiving turkey. "Leave him in peace. He's not going to hurt anyone." Jesse glared at Dave.

He studied Hank for a while, then shrugged. "You're probably right."

"So," Jesse said, wanting to hear the complete story, "you decided instead of getting a part time job that killing kids with drugs was a better way to go?"

"Now that part grieves me, Jesse." To Jesse's surprise, he looked genuinely repentant. "I don't want any of those kids to die, but I don't want to die either, and when it comes down to me or them, I win. Besides, they have a choice. They don't have to take the drugs. What choice did I have?"

That was the final straw. "You cold son of a—" Jesse took a step toward him.

"Uh uh. I wouldn't do that if I were you." The gun barrel moved from chest level to a direct line between Jesse's eyes.

Knowing Dave had spent many years hunting in these woods and that he was considered to be an ace marksman, Jesse took a cautious step backwards. Not a doubt lingered in his mind that Dave meant it. He would pull that trigger and not blink an eye.

And Jesse couldn't do Karen any good dead. He had to keep Dave talking until he could figure out how to get the gun and turn the tables on him.

"What about Hank? Why'd you kill him? What's he got to do with it?"

"Another one that couldn't leave well enough alone." Dave laughed. "I know you doubt it, but Hank felt as you did about Paul's death and was only trying to get rid of you to keep you out of danger. When he saw you coming up here yesterday he figured you were on to something, so he called me, and we came up here today see what you were looking for. He should have found you and Karen frozen to death or close to it, but I forgot that you almost lived in these caves since you were a kid." He shook his head. "Bad mistake on my part." He glanced at Hank's lifeless body. "But here we are. It all turned out okay in the end."

A fleeting stab of guilt for having suspected Hank was pushed aside by anger at what Dave seemed to think was fine. "Okay? Hank's dead. How can that be okay?"

Dave motioned to a large rock to Jesse's left. "Sit down. I'm an old man, and I can't stand around for long. Legs aren't what they used to be."

Jesse couldn't summon an ounce of sympathy for him. Despite the glaring sun, when Jesse sat down, the cold from the rock beneath him seeped through the material of his pants. The dried pine needles crunched beneath his feet and emitted the fragrance that Jesse had always equated with the peace of the forests. After this day, he was sure he wouldn't be able to smell that sweet pine scent without thinking about Hank's dead body and the cold barrel of a gun pointed at him by a man he'd called his friend.

How could he have misjudged Dave so badly? Jesse recalled Dave's willingness to talk with him about his problems, the days they'd spent together fishing and hunting until Jesse had come to see him as the father he'd never had, and then Dave's instant friendliness with Karen. He'd duped all of them: Karen, Hank, himself, and half the ranger station. That he'd fooled them all with his acts of kindness and concern for them made this seem ten times worse.

"Why is it your pretty friend didn't tag along with you?"

As though a wind straight out of the Antarctic had blown through, Dave's question jolted Jesse from his thoughts and turned his blood icy cold. He could not let Dave know where Karen was. After all, he'd planned on killing all three of them. "She went back to the city."

For a long time Dave stared at him, then he burst out laughing. "You must think me every kind of a fool to believe that. That little lady is in love with you. She's not going anywhere without you."

"You're wrong," Jesse all but yelled in his effort to convince Dave that Karen was far away from Bristol. "She's long gone. We had a fight, and I sent her packing. The last thing I need in my life right now is a woman clinging to me."

Again Dave studied Jesse, trying to read his expression. Jesse held his face blank. "Well, you'll pardon me if I don't believe you. You see, I saw how you looked at her. You're in love too, my boy. Head over heels. So you'd say anything to protect her. My guess is that she'll come after you so we'll just sit here a while and wait and see." He reached in the pocket of the bib overalls and pulled something out. The sun glinted off a metal object in Dave's hand.

The fear that had lain inside Jesse in a sick lump grew. Dave grinned as he brandished a lighter. "When she gets here, we're gonna have us a little marshmallow roast."

Jesse heard the sound of tires on gravel coming from the direction of the parking lot. His heart stopped and then started up at a breakneck speed. Fear unlike any he had ever experienced washed over him, turning his skin as cold as the ice in the caves. He glanced at Dave to see if he'd heard it, too.

"Seems we have company. Who do you suppose that could be?" His knowing sneer turned Jesse's stomach. "Nowadays, the women just can't resist playing the hero, showing us men up."

"Maybe it's not her," Jesse said, praying he was right. "It's probably just some tourist come to see the caves."

Dave stood and moved back behind a tree trunk that would hide him from Karen until it was too late. "Well, we'll soon see," he hissed at Jesse when he started to stand. "Make one false move, and I'll kill her before she can say her first word."

With a mixture of growing dread and fear churning inside him, Jesse stood stone still. Through the trees, he could see a spot of yellow. He repeated a silent prayer that it wasn't Karen. But as the spot grew larger, he realized it was the same color yellow as the blouse Karen had had on that morning.

Dammit, he'd told her to stay at the house. As he watched and the fear for her built, the spot grew larger and larger. When she finally stepped into the clearing, his heart dropped.

She spotted him instantly, and her expression brightened. "Jesse! Thank God." She rushed to him and threw her arms around him. As much as he wanted to, he made no move to hold her. She seemed not to notice his lack of response and stepped back. Excitement lit up her features. "We were wrong. It's not Hank. It's Dave, Jesse. Dave's the one trying to—" Something was terribly wrong. She stared questioningly at him. "What is it?"

Jesse's stony, totally unresponsive attitude numbed Karen's thought process. She waited for an answer, but Jesse just continued to stare over her shoulder. A rustling in the bushes behind her caught her attention. She swung toward the noise, and her breath gushed out of her.

Dave stood ten feet away with a gun aimed at them. "So glad you could join us, my dear, and how very clever of you to figure out it was me." He snapped the lighter open and then closed. The click echoed around the suddenly silent clearing. "You're just in time for the marshmallow roast."

Karen glanced at Jesse. "Marshmallow roast?"

His mouth was set in a grim line. "I think he plans on burning us up."

Karen felt her knees give way, but Jesse's arms slipped around her just in time to catch her. "He's going to—*what*?" The effect

Jesse's announcement had on her was betrayed further by her shaky voice.

Dave laughed. "You heard him right. I can't have anyone stumbling on your bodies and doing autopsies and finding anything to connect me to your deaths, now can I?"

"My sister's coming, and she's bringing the police," Karen blurted in a desperate attempt to stop him or at least prolong the implementation of the plans he had for them.

The second she felt Jesse stiffen against her, she realized her blunder and wished she could snatch the words back. Now Dave knew time was running out for him to do what he planned. She might as have put an *expedite* stamp on their deaths.

"They'll find Hank, Dave. His body will make them think twice that our deaths were accidental."

Dave frowned. "Hmm. I hadn't thought about that. Well, that's easily remedied. Good thing I took these from him before." He dug into his pocket, then threw Jesse a set of car keys. "Hank always carried his survival gear in his car. We'll just take a little walk over there and see if his backpack is in the trunk." Jesse glanced at Karen. "Oh, she'll be fine as long as you don't do anything stupid. Try anything," he pointed the gun at Karen's head, "and *bang*. She'll be dead."

Karen stared at Dave unable to equate this fiendish, heartless man with the one she'd come to care about. She felt Jesse stiffen as if preparing to pounce on Dave. She reached for his hand and gripped it tight. "No, Jesse. Don't do anything foolish. I'll be okay. Just do what he says."

Karen could feel Jesse hesitate. She held her breath. Then he squeezed her waist, and stepped around her. "Okay. Let's go."

She nodded and followed him into the bushes in the direction of the parking lot, but Dave grabbed her and kept her close to him, allowing Jesse to walk ahead of them. She could feel the hard barrel of the gun biting into her side. Gripping her hands together in front of her to keep them from shaking, she kept her gaze on Jesse's back and tried to draw strength from the fact that they were both okay and that they still had time to stop this. But how? She could only pray that Elle arrived with the posse soon.

When they reached the parking lot, Dave stopped Karen before she stepped from the cover of the bushes and let Jesse proceed to Hank's car. They remained there while Jesse rummaged through Hank's trunk to find the backpack.

From where they were, she couldn't see what Jesse was doing, but he seemed to be sorting through the trunk's contents.

"Hurry it up," Dave yelled.

It seemed hours before Jesse finally straightened and pulled the backpack from the car.

"I always said he was a smart boy," Dave whispered close to her ear and then motioned for Jesse to bring it.

Stepping to the side, he let Jesse go ahead of them before nudging Karen forward with the barrel of the gun. As Jesse passed them, his eyes shot pure hatred at Dave. Back in the clearing, Dave pushed Karen back to Jesse's side.

Jesse caught her around the waist and hugged her close. "You okay?"

Not sure she was, but seeing no need to add to Jesse's problems, she nodded. Her knees had stopped threatening to give out, but her hands still trembled. Determined not to give Dave the satisfaction of seeing her nervousness and fear, she jammed her hands in her pockets.

"Fine," she lied.

"Get out Hank's shovel and start digging," Dave instructed.

Realizing that he was making Jesse dig Hank's grave, Karen's stomach heaved. The hard set of Jesse's mouth told her he was not going to do this easily. She was right.

Jesse threw the shovel at Dave's feet. "Dig it yourself."

Dave made a *tsking* sound. "I just got finished saying how smart you are. But you're not being very smart now. Either you dig one grave . . ." he grabbed Karen and then raised the gun to her head, ". . . or you'll be digging two."

Despite the hot afternoon sun beating down on her, the cold

metal pressed against her temple sent chills down her spine. She could never remember being this scared, but she'd be damned before she showed him how frightened she was. She stiffened her spine and stared straight at Jesse, trying to tell him with her eyes that she was okay and to please do what Dave said.

He must have gotten the message because he picked up the shovel and started digging.

"Faster," Dave demanded gruffly. "If your girlfriend was telling the truth, we have company coming, and I don't want them interrupting our little marshmallow roast."

When the shallow grave was finally finished, Dave instructed Jesse to place Hank's body in it. Continuing to throw Dave hateful glances, Jesse did as he was told, then began shoveling dirt back in. It was a grim sight, one that Karen had to turn away from. Her heart broke for Jesse.

Despite everything, the bottom line was that Hank had not only been Jesse's boss, he'd also been his friend. To be the one to have to dig his grave and place him it must be torture for Jesse. She gritted her teeth and turned back, determined to show Jesse her support and understanding. It didn't matter because he never looked up from his chore.

When he'd finished replacing the dirt, Jesse chose a large, granite rock heavily veined with white quartz and placed it atop the freshly turned earth to mark Hank's final resting place. He straightened and looked at Karen. His cheeks were wet. He swiped at them with his shirttail and threw the shovel to the ground, then glared at Dave, his eyes overflowing with the loathing he felt for this man who had betrayed him and Hank.

Dave pushed Karen back toward Jesse. Jesse pulled her to him, taking some comfort from her closeness. "What now, old man?" He'd called Dave that many times over the years, but always in an affectionate way. This time it was as cold and as hard as steel.

"It's time for the marshmallow roast," Dave said flippantly, as if he were about to throw a birthday party.

Leering at Jesse and Karen, he walked to a large, granite rock and reached down behind it. What he pulled out was something Jesse had seen many times before, one of the drip cans they used to set backfires, probably the same one he'd used to set the fire that had killed Paul.

Holding the gun on them with one hand, Dave walked in a wide circle as he poured liquid from the can onto the ground. Instantly the overpowering smell of gasoline filled the air.

Jesse knew what was coming and had taken steps that he hoped would be enough to save Karen's life and his. When Dave ignited that gasoline, there would be little time to do anything.

"When I say *run*," he whispered in her ear, "don't hesitate. Follow me as fast as you can and do exactly what I say." Never taking her gaze from Dave, she nodded almost imperceptibly.

When he'd completed the circle, Dave moved far outside it and set the can down at his feet. He drew the lighter from his pocket and broke a dried out branch from a dead scrub pine tree and tucked it beneath the arm holding the gun so that it extended out in front of him. With all the flare of a magician doing his final trick, Dave flicked open the lighter, then held the flame to the branch. The dry wood burst into flame and for a scant moment the sweet smell of burning pine overpowered the odor of gas.

A breeze had kicked up. With it came both good and bad news. It would blow the fire through the area quickly, but perhaps too quickly for them to take the cover they needed.

Dave dropped the branch. As he did, a flaming twig broke off and landed near the gas can. The vapors ignited in a burst of flame and instantly spread to his clothes. Instantly, Dave's entire body was a pillar of red and orange flames. As he flailed about trying to put out the fire, his agonizing screams rent the air.

"Oh my God!" Karen's cry held more anguish than Jesse had ever heard before. She covered her eyes to shut out the horrendous sight.

Jesse forced himself to ignore it. He grabbed Karen, who was frozen in place repeating Dave's name over and over, and yelled,

"Run!"

He dragged her to where Hank's backpack lay. Digging into it, he pulled out the fire shelter he'd stuffed inside it when he'd gotten the shovel out of Hank's car, then threw the backpack as far from them as he could. Thanking Hank for his compulsive, repetitive training in the use of the fire shelter and the fact that Hank was a large man who required a super-sized version, Jesse deployed the shelter and pulled Karen inside it with him.

Pushing her onto her stomach, he spread his body on top of her, shielding her from the heat that would pass over them in seconds. Dave's screams were muffled now and after a few seconds, they went silent, and the only sound was the roar of the fire as it ate through the dry underbrush.

Jesse stretched out, using his feet to anchor the end of the shelter to prevent the fire's wind from catching it and blowing it up, exposing them to the flames and the heat. Then he slid his arms through the hold-down straps. He wrapped his arms around Karen, pressing as close to her as possible while he gathered the floor material in his hands to provide as good a seal as he could against the hot gases that would soon pass over them.

"Put your hands over your face," he instructed and pressed his face closer to her neck, then covered his cheeks with his own hands.

Outside they could hear the growl coming closer and closer.

Then the wildfire was on top of them.

Chapter 17

The air heated inside the shelter to an unbearable temperature almost instantly. It was stifling. Karen's skin felt as though it were on fire. Breathing became even more difficult with Jesse's weight pressing her into the hard ground.

Above her, Jesse groaned. Where her legs were without Jesse's protection, the material of her jeans absorbed the heat and burned against her skin. Since he was closer to the top of the shelter, she knew that the heat on his back had to be unbearable. She squirmed to get him closer to the ground.

"Keep still." His voice was laced with pain.

Her movements stilled instantly. She wished that there were some way she could protect Jesse, but there wasn't. They just had to wait it out and hope they survived.

Outside the shelter as the fire swept over them, the raging flames sounded like the scream of an enraged wild beast. Inside the shelter, the air grew more and more stifling. Karen fought for breath, but the heated air she did manage to suck into her lungs scorched her throat.

Nearby a tree crackled, then fell to the ground with a sickening thud that vibrated the ground beneath them. Thankfully, most of the trees in this area were small, but the ones that weren't, if they fell in the wrong direction, could crush them. She added one more terror to the host that had taken up residence inside her.

Then two explosions happening in quick succession drowned out the growl of the fire. The sound of metal bouncing off rocks and tress followed the explosion.

"Sounds like we just lost our transportation," Jesse said close to her ear.

151

Karen swallowed repeatedly to muffle the screams building in her throat.

Then, as suddenly as it had come upon them, the sounds outside the shelter began to fade. When it finally came, the silence was as deafening as the roar of the fire had been. She opened her eyes and looked into Jesse's face hovering inches from her own.

He smiled weakly. "I think we made it."

Without thinking, Karen threw her arms around his neck and kissed him. He grimaced, and then groaned.

She released him instantly. "You're hurt."

"We'll worry about that later," he said. "Let's get out of here." Jesse opened the shelter and crawled free. He took Karen's hand and pulled her up beside him. "Be careful where you step. There will be hot spots and the rocks retain the heat and will burn right through the soles of your shoes."

Everything smelled of burned wood and the smoke hung in heavy layers over the ground. Heat radiated up at them from the granite rocks. Karen looked around her at the blackened landscape. She couldn't believe they had actually survived. Paul and Dave hadn't and she couldn't even begin to imagine the agonizing deaths they'd endured.

"Let's get to the parking lot." Jesse took her hand and steered her through the burned tree stumps. At one point, he moved her to his other side. She was sure it was to keep her from seeing what remained of the man who had tried to kill them. Silently, she thanked Jesse.

Just as they stepped out of the bushes, a ranger vehicle pulled up beside them. Jesse was relieved to see Butch Haskell jump out.

"You two okay?"

Jesse nodded. "I think my back got a bit hot, but other than that, we're fine."

"The EMTs are right behind me. Butch motioned down the road leading up the mountain. "They'll see to your back."

"Your response time is improving, Haskell." Jesse grinned at the young ranger.

"The north tower spotted the smoke and then the flames, and we got a quick handle on the burn before it could turn into something uncontrollable. The guys should have it out before morning. The road just beyond Dave's cabin acted like a firebreak and stopped it from spreading down the mountain. Burned his cabin to the ground though. Lucky he wasn't home."

Jesse glanced at Karen, then back at Butch. "Dave's back there." He pointed behind them. "I think you'll find the drip can he used to start the fire beside him."

"Dave set the fire?"

Butch looked at Jesse as if he'd lost his mind, but Jesse ignored him. "In the clearing, you'll see a white rock. It's marking where Hank's body is buried. Dave killed him. We need to get him out of there and give him a proper burial."

Butch's mouth gaped, then he turned with what Jesse knew were questions hovering on the tip of his tongue. Again Jesse ignored him. A debilitating sadness sat heavy on his shoulders. He didn't want to think or talk about Hank or Dave or anything else. There would be plenty of time for that later when they rehashed it for the police. Right now, he wanted to get away from this place and all its miserable memories.

"You'll get all the information later, Butch."

As if answering his need, the EMT's drove into the parking lot. Using the need for first aid as an excuse, Jesse took Karen's arm and led her toward the truck.

After the EMTs had treated Jesse's back for minor burns, he climbed out of the EMT truck just in time to see four of his fellow rangers carry two black body bags from the direction of the caves. His throat growing tight, he turned away and fought the tears that threatened to fill his eyes.

He still couldn't believe that Dave had turned on him. But the proof lay in the burned out forest around him, the charred wrecks of Hank's car and his, and the stinging burns on his back. He just wished he'd had time to tell Hank he was sorry for ever doubting him. Looking toward the blinding blue heavens, he had to believe that Hank knew. He had to. It was the only way Jesse could live with himself.

He looked around for Karen, but she was nowhere in sight. When they'd reached the EMT's truck, they'd taken him inside immediately to treat his burns, and he'd lost track of her.

"Have you seen Karen?" he asked Butch.

Butch pointed toward the back of one of the fire trucks parked around the busy lot. Jesse could make out Karen climbing into her car with Elle and closing the door. The car made a wide U-turn and disappeared down the road off the mountain.

Jesse felt as though he'd been sucker-punched. She hadn't even stayed long enough to find out if he was okay. Maybe she didn't care. Maybe she just wanted to be free of this place as much as he did. Or maybe she just wanted to be free of him.

His stomach clenched and a pain shot through him. Since his car lay in a charred tangle of metal, he couldn't even go after her. But did she want him to?

"Are you sure you don't want to wait for Jesse to get home?" Karen and Elle stood side by side in the driveway to Jesse's house watching Scott put Karen's suitcases in the trunk of her sporty red car.

"No. There's no point, Elle. He's made it very clear that he wants me gone. It'll be easier on both of us if I just go now."

Scott slammed the trunk closed, took the keys from the lock and handed them to Karen. "Drive carefully," he said, then kissed her cheek. He patted Elle's flat stomach and grinned. "Scott Jr is looking forward to meeting his cousin." He kissed Elle, then sauntered off to their rental car, leaving Elle and Karen alone to say their goodbyes.

"What about Paul's family?" Elle asked. "Will you keep looking for them?"

Karen gazed across the field at Emily's house. The faint sounds of the twins' laughter drifted to them. How she would have loved for her child to know this family, to bask in their closeness and love. But that was not to be.

She shrugged and smiled at Elle. "He or she will have you, Scott, Dad, and pretty soon a brand new cousin. That should be enough family for any kid."

"Absolutely." Elle hugged her. "We'll expect to see you in Florida soon." She hugged Karen, kissed her cheek, and then took a step away. "I'm really gonna miss you."

"Me, too." Karen choked back her tears and gave her sister a playful shove. "You better get out of here before we get too maudlin."

With a heavy heart, she watched Elle get into the car, then stared after the car until it disappeared from sight. Everything in her wanted to call Elle back, but she laid her palm against her stomach and whispered, "Time to go, sweetheart."

She'd opened her car door when the sound of another car in the driveway stopped her. Thinking Elle had forgotten something, she grinned and turned toward the vehicle, a teasing comment about Elle's lapse in memory hovering on her lips.

When she saw that it was not Elle, but a forestry vehicle, and who drove it, the smile faded abruptly, the playful retort instantly forgotten. Jesse exited the car and walked purposefully toward her, his lips set in a thin, angry line. He limped slightly on his injured ankle. Karen steeled herself against the urge to run to him and beg him to ask her to stay.

Instead, she kept her expression neutral and said, "How's your back?" she asked.

"Forget my back." He pushed the car door closed. "Why did you leave?"

"I thought it would be best."

"Best for who?"

"Both of us." Unable to bear him being so close, yet so untouchable, Karen kept her gaze fixed over Jesse's shoulder.

He looked at the sky, trying to keep his anger in check. With his fists clenched in his pockets, he stepped in front of her line of vision, forcing her to look him in the eye. "For both of us? I don't have any say in this?"

Swallowing her pride, she returned his gaze. "Do you want me to stay, Jesse?"

Dammit, he didn't want her to go. He loved her. But even faced with her leaving, Jesse still couldn't free his emotions from the cage he'd kept them in for so long. What if she stayed and regretted it like his mother had? He'd never forgive himself for screwing up her life to satisfy his selfish needs. He couldn't stand it if she ended her life as a bitter woman forced to live a life she didn't want.

She shifted her weight, and her car keys jingled, rousing him from his thoughtful stupor. Although everything in him told him to grab her and never let her go, he still couldn't say the words that would keep her there.

The silence stretched out into more long, uncomfortable moments. She sighed. "Well, I guess that answers my question."

Without another word, Karen got into her car, closed the door and started the engine. She glanced at him briefly out her side window, then put the car in reverse and backed out of the driveway.

Jesse stood there as his life disappeared down the road, helpless to stop her. No matter how many excuses he made, in his heart he knew that letting her go had nothing to do with how his mother had hated the country or that he had never told Karen about Paul's marriage. It had everything to do with him and his fear of loving and losing.

Or never being loved at all.

The following days passed for Jesse on slow-dragging feet, each harder to face than the last. He'd attended Hank's funeral and then come home to an empty house that taunted him with residual memories of Karen's presence. He'd made a trip to his beloved woods, a place that had never failed to bring him peace, a place where he always found solace for life's troubles in the arms of

Mother Nature. But the peace he searched for remained elusive. All he had found were more haunting memories of the day he and Karen had made love on a blanket beneath the sheltering branches of the towering pines. Even going back to the job he loved held no appeal for him.

He had to do something. Otherwise he'd just keep slipping deeper and deeper into a black hole of depression. And that there was only one thing that could throw him a lifeline—Karen. He had to go see her and hope he could open up enough to make her understand. The decision seemed to remove some of the weight he'd been carrying around on his shoulders since Karen had left.

A knock at his back door dragged him from his thoughts. It was still early morning on a Sunday. He hadn't slept more than a handful of hours the night before. The last thing he needed right now was company, and he thought about ignoring whoever was standing on his porch. But his car was in the driveway.

Slowly, he got to his feet and went to answer the knock. Swinging the door open, he froze in place with his mouth open.

On the porch stood Emily, Diane and Iris. All three bore a look of determination that told him they were on a mission, and he was not going to get rid of them easily.

"Hi," Jesse said, wondering what they were doing on his doorstep at eight in the morning.

"Hello, brother dear." Emily pushed past him into the kitchen. Diane and Iris followed on her heels. "Ladies, let's do it," she instructed, ignoring Jesse as though he were just a part of the furniture.

Like soldiers obeying their commanding officer, Iris marched to the table where she deposited the cake carrier she'd brought with her, then started searching the cabinets, Jesse assumed for plates. When Emily headed for the coffeemaker, Diane intercepted her and took over the task of brewing coffee. Emily threw her a look of feigned indignation and found silverware and coffee cups, then set the table. Jesse could only stare in openmouthed amazement.

"Sit," Diane commanded in a no-nonsense tone and pointed at one of the kitchen chairs. Jesse obeyed as readily as a troop of soldiers facing a drill instructor.

After watching his relatives bustle about his kitchen for a few more minutes, Jesse finally found his voice. "Is anyone going to tell me what's going on here?"

Iris glanced away from her cake-cutting chore and grinned. "I believe the technical name for it is an intervention, but we're gonna call it a *come-to-Jesus* meeting."

When all three women had finished their respective chores, they gathered around the table and stared at him.

"What?" he finally asked when no one spoke.

"Diane," Emily said, "you go first."

All eyes turned to Diane. "Like it or not, Jesse Kingston, we're your family."

Jesse opened his mouth to say he never denied that they were his family, but the words never got past his lips. Emily's glare stopped them cold.

"As I was saying . . . we're your family. When family has a problem, they confide in each other." She shook her finger at him as though she were reprimanding Danny for some mischief. "We've been very patient with you, brother."

"That's right," Emily chimed in and as if scripted, Diane let her sister resume the conversation.

What had started out as annoying to Jesse quickly became amusing. His sisters had never ganged up on him before, except for the time they took away the ladder and left him stranded in the apple tree behind the house. That little bit of underhanded play had, much to Jesse's surprise, even dragged a faint smile from his stone-faced father.

"It hasn't gone beyond our notice that ever since Karen left you've closeted yourself here and moped around like an old hound dog that's lost the scent," Emily continued.

"As we see it, you can do one of two things, son," Iris told him in her best *mother-will-take-no-prisoners* voice. Evidently, this was her part of the show. Jesse listened as the older woman ticked off his choices on her fingers. "One, you can pull up your boxer shorts, forget her and get on with your life. Or two, you can swallow your pride and go after her and beg her forgiveness for whatever stupid male thing you did that upset her enough to leave without even saying goodbye to us."

"That's it?" he said, looking from one to the other.

"That's it," they affirmed in unison.

Emily laid her hand on his. Her eyes welled with moisture. "We love you, and we want you to be happy, Jesse. You've had so little happiness in your life. When we met Karen, we saw the look on your face. You're in love. Besides," she said, obviously trying to lighten the mood, "we took a vote, and we want her as part of the family." Diane and Iris nodded their agreement.

Unable to hold his somber face any longer, Jesse laughed, and it felt good. "It may interest all of you to know that I had already decided to go to Karen before you barged in here like a battalion of Patton's foot soldiers."

They at least had the good grace to look embarrassed. "Oh, well," Diane said, "better late than never." They all nodded and laughed.

Suddenly, Jesse wanted them to know how special he thought they all were to him and how much he appreciated their caring. "You guys are the best. I love you all very much." Once the words were out, he realized how little it had taken to say them and how very much he meant every one of them. Why couldn't he have done that with Karen?

"As much as we appreciate your declaration of affection, I think those are words you should be saying to Karen." Iris said, rubbing her hands together like she was about to execute a complicated CIA maneuver. "So, what can we do to help you win her back?"

Jesse glanced at the cake sitting on the cabinet. 'Well, first of all, you can give me a slice of that cake and a cup of Diane's coffee." The words had barely passed over his lips when Iris was on her feet slicing cake, and Diane had grabbed the coffee pot and filled everyone's cup.

When they were all settled at the table again and Jesse had wolfed down several forkfuls of Iris' cake, Diane posed the same question Iris had earlier. "What can we do to help?"

Jesse though for a while, then said, "I need the use of a computer. Any of you have one?"

Emily and Diane turned immediately to Iris. "All right, so I'm a computer game addict." Iris blushed and turned her concentration to pushing the cake crumbs around her plate with her fork.

"Great! I need to look up an address or two in your computer white pages." When he looked up, all three were staring at him waiting for his further explanation.

"Does this have anything to do with the baby Karen's expecting?"

Iris's question almost knocked him off his chair. "How did you know she's expecting?"

Emily laughed and stood to gather their plates. "She figured it out the day of the barbeque. Don't ask me how she does it. She knew I was expecting the twins before I told her, too." She leaned down by his ear and in a stage whisper said, "She's a dear, and I love her like a mother, but sometimes, she's just a tad weird."

"I heard that," Iris exclaimed.

For a time Jesse said nothing, just sat back and listened to the good-natured banter amongst the women in his life. How much he'd missed out on by holding himself away from them.

Well, as of today, he vowed, that was at an end. He was through being an emotional recluse.

As the four of them cleaned up the kitchen, Jesse related what he knew of Karen's relationship with Paul and Paul's death. Leaving nothing out except the day he and Karen had spent in the pine grove, he told them everything, right up to the day at the caves with Dave. When the kitchen was again spotless, they escorted Jesse across the field to Emily's so Jesse could begin the search for Paul's family's address. The sooner he found them, the sooner he could go to Karen.

Karen stared out her fourth-story window at the apartment building across the street. How she hated the lack of wide-open space, the fast pace, and the constant clamor of the city now. Bristol had spoiled her, and she longed for the peace and quiet she'd found there.

Even more, she longed for Jesse. There had only been a few mornings that she'd sat across the breakfast table from him at his house, but now, the pain of facing an empty chair, forced her to bring her morning coffee into the living room. But even that didn't erase his image from her mind or the love she had for him from her heart.

She stroked her tummy. Since she'd come home, it had expanded to the point of making it impossible not to start wearing maternity clothes. The sonogram she'd had last week had revealed that she was going to have a boy. How wonderful it would have been for him to have grown up with Jesse as his dad.

The pain of such thoughts was just too much for her to bear. The hurt went too deep. There was no sense in longing for something beyond her grasp.

She'd learned that the hard way. After she got home from Bristol, she'd cried enough tears to end her up in the ER of the local hospital. Her doctor had sternly admonished her that, for the baby's sake, she had to start keeping her nerves under control. When she'd come home, she'd vowed to do just that, but thoughts of Jesse had a way of slipping under her guard all too often, and she had trouble erasing them.

Oddly, the daylight hours were the worst. Since she'd never shared his bed, the expectation of him lying next to her on waking never came. But during the day, when she least expected, she'd recall walking through the woods with him, making love with him while the birds sang above them, feeling his skin on hers, his hoarse voice whispering in her ear . . . .

She shook her mind free, but the shadows of what could have

been remained. In the end, to cleanse her mind of the torturing thoughts of Jesse, she picked up a book of baby names she'd gotten at the neighborhood bookstore and began leafing through it. Before long, she was deeply engrossed in trying out names for the baby . . . the baby she wished she and Jesse could have raised together.

Jesse stood outside the door of apartment 412. Karen's apartment. He raised his fist to knock, then dropped it back to his side. His stomach felt as if a kaleidoscope of butterflies had taken up residence.

What if she turned him down? What if she wouldn't even talk to him? What if she didn't love him as Iris swore Karen did because she'd read it in her eyes? What if Iris had told him that because she knew it was what he'd wanted to hear?

Questions and doubts hammered at his mind. Then Emily's words filtered through the tangle of misgivings.

Life only comes with a reasonable expectation of happiness and the human ability to find it. Believe me, it's well worth the risks.

Raising his fist again, he knocked, then waited. Seconds later, the door opened. Karen's shocked face stared back at him.

"Jesse? What are you doing here?"

"I need to talk to you." She made no move to invite him in. "Please." Still she didn't move. "Karen?"

She started as though waking from a dream. "Uh, about what?"

"May I come in?"

"I'm sorry. Of course. Come in." She stepped to the side, and he noted that her pregnancy had become much more noticeable. She closed the door behind him and motioned him into a small living room. "Please, sit."

He did. For a moment, he could only hungrily drink in the sight of her. She was still breathtakingly beautiful, maybe more so now that the bloom of motherhood had magnified. Her green eyes appeared brighter. Her hair, pulled back in a ponytail, made her cheeks and heart-shaped face more prominent.

She moistened her lips. His stomach knotted painfully. "What was it you wanted to talk about?"

Jesse reached in his pocket and extracted a small sheet of paper. "Before I give you this, there's something you need to know about Paul, something I haven't told you."

She sat silent, her expression guarded, but at the same time expectant.

For a very long moment, Jesse stared at the piece of paper trying to find the right words. Then he lifted his gaze to meet hers, his brow furrowed in thought. "Karen did you ever wonder why Paul never talked about his family or where he came from?"

She shrugged. "I always assumed he just didn't want to. I mean, I wasn't what you'd call forthcoming about my family either. It was kind of an unspoken agreement, he didn't ask and neither did I."

He rubbed his eyes. "Damn." His demeanor told her that he would have rather been discussing anything but this. "Karen, Paul never talked about his family to you because . . . because he couldn't. He was married."

The words hit her in the gut with all the force of a freight train. *Paul—married?*

Karen closed her eyes. She felt as though someone had chopped a hole in the floor beneath her and sent her spiraling down into a bottomless, dark hole.

Humiliation sapped her of the ability to speak. What Jesse must think of her. That she would not only have a relationship with a married man, but that she'd allow herself to get pregnant with his child. No wonder he'd wanted her to leave.

She raised her gaze and met his. "I didn't know. I swear, I did not know."

He left the chair he'd been sitting in and joined her on the couch. "Don't you think I know that? My ears are still burning from the talking to you gave me about getting to know my nieces and letting my family in. Anyone who feels like that could not possibly have gotten involved with a man who already had a family and take the chance of ruining that family." He took her chin in his hand and turned her face to him. "Karen, you were not to blame. Paul should have told you."

Her shoulders slumped. "Thank God I never found his family," she mumbled. "I could have destroyed them."

He encircled them with his arm and pulled her close to him. "If it makes this any easier to take, I just found out that Paul and his wife were legally separated when he met you. There was nothing to destroy." He held up the scrap of paper. "This is her address." He placed it in Karen's hand and curled her fingers over it.

She stared down at it. "Did you . . . did you tell her about—"

"The baby? No. I saw no reason to. Paul has no other living relatives, no siblings, no aunts or uncles, and his parents passed away a few years ago within months of each other." He laid his hand on her tummy. "She's all yours."

"He."

"What?"

"The baby's a _he_. A boy."

Jesse grinned. "That's great!"

She smiled up at him, her eyes watery. "Yes, it is, isn't it?" Then she took the piece of paper containing Paul's wife's address and tore it into tiny pieces.

Jesse frowned. "You're not going to use it?"

Karen shook her head and threw the pieces in a wastebasket. "She has no need to know that Paul betrayed her. Let her get on with her life."

One more proof that Karen had insight into other people and cared for them beyond anything Jesse had ever seen before. It was time he took the plunge and did what he'd come here for.

"Karen, speaking of getting on with life . . . I need to apologize for the way I treated you the last few days you were in Bristol." She kept her gaze turned from him. He lifted her chin and made her face him. "I was a jerk. I thought I could protect you from Dave by getting you to go home." He cupped both sides of her face with his hands. "I never wanted you to leave. Never. I love you."

A smile spread across her face. "Why didn't you tell me that? Why, even after it was over, didn't you stop me from leaving?"

He shook his head. "It sounds so silly now, but I was afraid you'd turn me down. I was afraid you wouldn't want to live in Bristol. I was afraid, when you found out about Paul's marriage, you'd hate me for keeping it from you. I was afraid . . . Oh hell, I was afraid of your love."

"Afraid of my love? Why would you be afraid of my love?"

Slowly, Jesse told her about his mother and how much she hated the country. How she'd taken her young son and run back to the city she loved, leaving behind a bitter man. Then about the stoic man he'd called *father*, and how he'd thrown Jesse's love back at him. How he'd loved Jesse's mom so much that he couldn't stand the sight of a son that reminded him of her. And finally, Jesse's fear of becoming his father.

Karen gasped. "Jesse, you are not that man. You're kind, caring and compassionate. If you were like your father, I couldn't—" She smiled and leaned forward, then kissed him. Then she wrapped her arms around his neck and whispered in his ear. "I couldn't have fallen in love with you."

Jesse held her tight. He felt as though some unseen power had handed him more happiness than any man should be allowed to have in one lifetime.

Then he recalled something Paul said to him after they'd survived their first wildfire.

There are no stronger relationships than those bound by fire.

Epilogue

Karen stood on the top step leading down to the patio and gazed out on the gathering below her. A sea of people milled about carrying drinks and sandwiches. As her gaze searched the crowd of family, she easily found the man she'd been seeking. Jesse was deep in conversation with his sister, one of the baby's godmothers, Emily. In his arms, despite the din going on around him, Kelley slept soundly.

As though Jesse felt her gaze come to rest on him, he raised his head and smiled at her. She threw him a kiss and walked toward him. He separated himself from the heart of the crowd and made his way to her.

Karen couldn't have asked for a better dad for her son . . . *their* son. Since the baby's birth two months earlier, Jesse seldom strayed far from his side. When he came home, he kissed her hello and then checked on Kelley. When Kelley awoke in the night, Jesse was often there before Karen could fully open her eyes. When she nursed Kelley, Jesse cradled her close while the boy ate.

"I think the honored guest has pooped out on his own party," Jesse said, smiling down at the cherubic face. "Want me to put him to bed?"

"You spoil me." On tiptoe, she kissed his mouth with a promise of more to come later.

He returned the kiss and accepted her promise. "What's a husband for?"

"Put him in the cradle in our room. Elle and Scott just put baby Martha down in the nursery." Jesse nodded and moved off toward the back porch. "Hurry back. With Kelley snoozing, it'll be up to us to entertain his guests until he wakes up."

She watched him go through the door then turned back to the party. A contented sigh issued from her. She'd so wanted a family for Kelley and herself. Now, they had more family than she'd ever dared dream of. Elle, Scott, baby Martha, and her dad would have been enough. But when she'd married Jesse, with him came Iris, Emily, Kat, the twins, Diane, Lou, and Danny and in a few months, another precious baby would be born to Diane and Lou. Kelley had more than enough aunts, uncles and cousins for any little boy.

And she had Jesse.

Suddenly, she wanted to be with her husband. Throwing a glance at the crowd to make sure everything was going well, she re-entered the house and made her way to their room. As she drew close to the bedroom doorway, she could hear Jesse talking low. Peeking in, she saw Jesse lying beside Kelley on the bed. Stepping back and standing out of sight around the corner, she listened to her husband talk to the baby.

"You don't know it, but today you officially became my son. Not that I didn't think of you like that already. You're as much a part of me as your mom is. You both are my life, and I'll never do anything to make you doubt that. Every day, I'll tell you how much I love you, so you'll never have to wonder.

"That doesn't mean that we'll forget your biological dad. We won't. When you're old enough, I'll tell you all about him. You'd have liked him a lot. He was a very brave man, and a very good friend who died because he was trying to do what was right and honorable. You're a very lucky little boy to have his blood flowing through your veins."

He stopped talking for a moment. Karen peeked around the door in time to see him kiss the baby's forehead, then lean back against the pillows and close his eyes.

"Then there's your mom. Shall I tell you about her? She's a very special lady. No one has ever understood me like she does and been able to see what's in my heart. If it hadn't been for her, I'd still be living in a cold, dark place, unwarmed by her love. It took me a long time to learn to let myself love anyone, but now, my entire being is filled with love for her."

Karen's eyes welled up, and she slipped into the room. Quietly she made her way to the side of the bed, leaned down and kissed Jesse with all the emotion his words had brought to life.

"I love you, Jesse Kingston. More than you'll ever believe."

Beside them, Kelley stirred, opened his eyes and smiled.

———

Read on for a preview of Elizabeth's new series . . . .

The Survivors

Preview: *The Survivors*

New Series!
Coming soon from Elizabeth Sinclair
and Salt Run Publishing LLC

MEET THE SURVIVORS
Charlene "Charlie" Donovan – former FBI computer tech
Melina Spanaes – former NYC detective
Linda Webb – arson investigator
Haley Conlan – forensics specialist

Each of these women has survived a horrendous event in their lives and each has sworn to pursue criminals and procure justice for victims and their families. They've been called together by Charlene Donovan to uphold that oath. Because of *The Survivors'* overwhelming success in helping to solve cases, the governor has made them a special task force attached to the New York State Troopers.

Blood on the Ashes

Prologue

She could smell the acrid smoke and hear the crackle before she woke up fully and saw her terrifying nightmare was all too real. Frozen in terror, she clutched the blankets around her chin and stared at the flickering orange light beneath her bedroom door.

As she watched, like the fingers of a child begging for entry, the flames curled under the wooden barricade and slowly climbed toward the ceiling. With its admittance, a searing heat slowly began to fill the room.

The rising temperature jarred her from her paralyzed state. If she didn't get out, she was going to die. She clambered from the bed and ran to the window. The floor was oddly cold beneath her bare feet. Bracing her hands on the window's frame, she pushed up, but it wouldn't budge. The humidity of the last few rainy summer days had swollen the wood. Acutely aware of the growth of the encroaching flames, she tried again and again without success. She pounded her fist against the window frame until the skin broke and blood ran down her wrist and dripped onto the floor.

And the heat increased. The flames climbed the wall like a many-headed, large orange snake, slithering and winding from side to side and devouring everything it touched.

Desperate, she grabbed a perfume bottle off the dresser and smashed the pane. Glass splintered. A few shards came back into the room. One large piece embedded itself in her instep. Oblivious to the pain, she yanked it out and threw it across the room. Blood ran over her foot and pooled on the floor.

Turning back to the broken window, she searched the night for help. She could just make out the shadow of someone walking down the driveway.

She pounded on the window frame and screamed to the person below through the broken pane. "Help! Please help me!"

But the shadowy figure kept walking, and then disappeared into the night, and the only sounds she could hear were her sobs and the crackle of the fire devouring the room she'd slept in since childhood. When she turned back to the fire, she knew her attempt to escape had done more harm than good. The new supply of oxygen had only served to feed the hungry blaze. Her terror morphed instantly to bone-chilling horror.

The fire had started to spread across the ceiling. She'd dated a fireman, and she remembered him talking about a flashover. She knew that the fire would fan out across the ceiling and, without touching anything below, would radiate so much heat that everything in the room would be ignited—including her. Soon both she and the room would be an inferno.

She had to get out. But how? Trying to push back her panic, she turned back to the window. While she screamed for help, she began breaking out the remaining shards of glass with the perfume bottle, hoping she could make the opening large enough to crawl through.

But the fire had other plans for her and before she could even think about escaping through the window, with a loud whoosh, the bed burst into flames. As she watched in abject terror, her nightgown became a shroud of fire. Screams erupted from her dry throat and were instantly absorbed in the roar of the fire devouring the remains of the room. The last thing that registered in her mind was a sharp pain in her left temple and the smell of her own flesh cooking.

On a hill near the tennis court, a hooded figure stepped from behind a tree, shouldered the rifle, and then strolled slowly away from the house. Pausing for a moment, the shooter looked back at the conflagration, smiled, and then faded into the shadows of the trees.

About The Author

ELIZABETH SINCLAIR admits she loved composition assignments back in grade school. While other kids glared at the teacher, she was always excited at the prospect of creating a new story in a new world. However, it wasn't until her own children were all in school—and the house remained clean for more than a few minutes at a time—that she found the time to really write.

Throughout Elizabeth's lengthy career, her romance writing has evolved into romantic suspense involving complex characters, intricate plots, and heart-racing stories that fellow author Sharon Drane once stated, "Cannot be read alone, at night."

Elizabeth's books have won The National Reader's Choice Award, The Anne Bonney Reader's Choice Award, Romantic Times Reviewer's Choice Award, Maggie Award of Excellence, and placed in the Heart of Excellence. She has also won a Gold Medal Top Pick from the Romantic Times Book Club.

Elizabeth is a co-founder and member of the Ancient City Romance Authors of St. Augustine, FL, a member of Romance Writers of America, and served as RWA's Region 3 Director and chaired the 2001 RWA Annual Conference in New Orleans.

Elizabeth shares her Florida home with her husband and their furry children. Her human family has expanded to include five grandchildren and one great-granddaughter.

About the Cover Designer

Stacey Sather is a freelance designer & artist who has become impassioned with the art of creative photography.

With 25+ years of experience in commercial design, she is now enjoying the opportunity to circle back and blend her fine art training, design and photographic talents for an entirely new venture.

Born in the hamlet of Cragsmoor, NY, and having lived in various regions of the U.S., she feels fortunate to call the captivating city of St. Augustine, Florida "home".

Follow Stacey on her photo-exploration of her travels and of the "Nations Oldest City" as she shares her images of its beauty, history and cultural allure.

For more information or to contact Stacey, visit www.sgsdesignandart.com, or email SGSdesign@mac.com.